RISE OF THE MAGE

RISE OF THE MAGE

RESURRECTING MAGIC - BOOK ONE

USA TODAY BESTSELLING AUTHOR
KEARY TAYLOR

Copyright © 2020 Keary Taylor

All rights reserved. Except as permitted under the U.S. Copyright act of 1976, no part of this publication may be reproduced, distributed, or transmitted in any form or by any means, or stored in a database or retrieval system, without the prior written permission of the author.

First Edition: March 2020

Cover art by Orina Kafe

The characters and events portrayed in this book are fictitious. Any similarity to real persons, living or dead, is coincidental and not intended by the author.

Taylor, Keary, 1987-

Rise of the Mage (Resurrecting Magic): a novel / by Keary Taylor. – 1st ed.

ALSO BY KEARY TAYLOR

THE BLOOD DESCENDANTS UNIVERSE

House of Royals Saga

Garden of Thorns Trilogy

Crown of Death Saga

THE FALL OF ANGELS TRILOGY

THE NERON RISING SAGA

THE EDEN TRILOGY

THE McCAIN SAGA

WHAT I DIDN'T SAY

Also by T.L. Keary (thriller/suspense pen name)

THREE HEART ECHO

OUR LAST CONFESSION

SKIN AND BONE

CHAPTER ONE

As I stood in front of the main doors, I wondered if, somehow, I was missing something in this whole experience. I watched dozens of others racing through the doors or across the perfectly manicured lawns, their eyes wide, maybe a little panicked. Some looked exceptionally ambitious. Most were excited.

I wasn't feeling the same things they were.

I wasn't feeling nervous. I didn't feel lost. I wasn't excited to be in a new place.

I just felt comfortable.

Maybe even a tiny bit bored.

My eyes studied the façade of Alderidge University. I'd heard it described as a cross between a castle and a Southern plantation. Something that had been born of both Scottish and Mississippi parents. A mix of rock and brick climbed up its face. Great pillars held up the overhang of the main doors. There were four main spires along the front of the building. Over the years, more buildings had been added, all grouped together in 150 square acres along the edge of the water here in Harrington, Massachusetts.

It was all beautiful, except for the north wing, which had been damaged by a storm and then a fire twenty years ago, and no one had ever bothered to fix it.

I knew I was lucky to attend. Alderidge was a prestigious university. I was grateful to be here.

But here was where I'd been every day for my entire life.

"Margot." The most familiar voice in my whole world startled me. I turned, my bag slung over my shoulder, and found my father walking up, coming from the direction I'd just come. "Not going to give me a bad reputation on your first day, are you? Can't have the daughter of a professor not showing up on time."

A little smile pulled on my lips. "Have I *ever* done *anything* to embarrass you?" I asked, giving him a look.

"Well, you *are* eighteen," he said, a controlled smile pulling on his face. "I hear this is the usual time for young people to begin rebelling." Except he knew me, and the look on his face told me he never wondered if I'd go off the deep end.

I gave him a smile. "Come on," I said, inclining my head to the doors. "You can walk me to my first class."

His eyes shone with appreciation, but he held it together well, and just gave a nod. Side-by-side, we stepped forward, down the cobbled pathway to the front doors.

With the weather still perfect at the end of August, the others around me wore skirts and long stockings, thin button-ups, and linen trousers. The skin would soon disappear, and we would all be wearing thick coats, scarves, hats, and gloves. Anything to combat the chill of New England winters.

But for now, every one of us was enjoying the fair weather.

"Morning," I greeted Professor Garrett, my father's closest friend. He rushed down the hall, but offered a quick smile and a dramatic, overwhelmed expression to draw a laugh from both of us. And right behind him was Professor Rogers, who gave me a quick hug and a wish for good luck.

None of these other students knew anything about their professors, yet I considered half of them friends, and the other half had known me since I was just a little girl following my parents around campus.

I knew exactly where I was going when I turned left down a hallway and aimed for the second door on the left. I stopped in the doorway, adjusted the bag slung over my shoulder and looked up at my dad.

Professor Arthur Bell had my same sandy blonde hair and the same ever-so-slight dip in his chin. But while my eyes were blue, his were green. My nose was button shaped, and his was long. The crow's feet in the corners of his eyes were getting longer by the night. I told him it was because of his habit of reading by candlelight, despite it being the twentieth century. The squinting was making him age.

"I'd say good luck, but I know you're already going to embarrass every other student in there," Dad said, his eyes roving over my face. "I'm still angry with Laurence that he wouldn't advance you."

"She's still a freshman," Laurence called from within the classroom.

"Who's known Latin since she was twelve," my dad called back to his friend. There was real irritation in his voice.

"Freshman!" Laurence called back.

I just chuckled and shook my head, in almost exactly the same way my father did. "It's okay. Since when is having an easy semester a bad thing?"

My dad shook his head and pulled me into a hug. Yes, my face flushed a little at that, and my eyes darted around, noting all the other students witnessing this father-daughter moment.

I didn't care that much. But I did care a little.

"Well, you've already got an honorary degree, in my opinion," my dad said, squeezing me just once more before he released me. With a firm grip on my upper arms, he looked me in the eyes. "I'm proud of you, Margot. You're going to destroy them all."

I huffed a little laugh, shaking my head at him. But I smiled in appreciation, then watched as he walked away, down the hall, his leather briefcase, the same one he'd had since I was a toddler, clutched in his left hand.

I watched four other students walk into the classroom. All freshman, all similar eighteen- and nineteen-year-olds, ready to start the next four years of their lives.

I let out one deep breath and stepped into the class to join my peers.

Latin, Writing, and Social Studies comprised my classes for the day. Mondays, Wednesdays, and Fridays were my heavier days. Tuesdays and Thursdays were for my elective classes, World Geography and Physical Education.

By my first Friday evening as a college student, I had four homework assignments to work on.

I'd made zero friends yet.

Not that I'd ever been very good at that.

My parents always said I had an old soul. I wondered if that was true or if it was simply because I'd grown up as the only child of two university professors. I'd never been given the chance to be around other kids, so that had made it difficult to make friends with people my own age.

Middle school was horrific. High school had gotten slightly easier. I made a few good friends, my circle small, but tight.

But then we all graduated school. We all headed in different directions. And I was the only one who stayed here and went to Alderidge.

I was back at square one, feeling like an outsider in my own age group.

So, while others around me talked about going to parties and their weekend plans to go to the beach, I gathered my homework, put it in my bag, and headed to the library.

It was located at the back of the University. Right in the middle of the main building, to me, it was the heart and soul of the school that had been around since 1723, nearly two and a half centuries old. As I stepped through the central set of doors, I stopped for just a moment, taking it in.

The study space was set centrally. Three lines of tables, eight rows deep. Huge chandeliers hung over the outside rows of tables. Once upon a time, they held candles. I wondered how they ever lit them, they were so exceptionally high. But now they'd been converted for electricity and used lightbulbs.

Wood beams stretched throughout the vaulted space. Toward the back was the circulation desk, where the librarians helped students find what was needed. The desk was old, a huge thing made of oak. Just behind it, was a massive stained-glass window that looked out at the Atlantic Ocean and cast streaks of light throughout the entire space.

Stacks of bookshelves branched off from the study area. At first in neat rows, dozens deep. But there had been wings added over the years. Entire rooms just for poetry or history books. Offices that once housed some of the world's most renowned scholars were now converted to individual libraries or reservable study rooms. There were spiral staircases rising up to the second floor, where there were even more books, all stacked on wooden shelves far older than even Professor Campbell.

Goosebumps rose on my arms as I took it all in.

This was my world.

This was where I found myself. Where I found what I wanted to do for the rest of my life.

I could spend an entire day lost in a book and it would be a day well spent. I'd gotten lost in new worlds and old fairy tales. I knew every myth and legend of the Greeks and Egyptians.

I loved stories. Old and new.

I smiled as I stepped inside and made my way through the study tables, back to the section I knew would hold the volume I looked for.

There were others here. I wasn't the only student studying instead of playing. This was Alderidge, after all. You didn't get in unless you had exceptional study habits and a sharp mind. So I wasn't surprised to find a dozen others spread throughout the tables, another dozen or so visible as they wandered through the stacks of books.

While other schools had fraternities and sororities, we had the Society Boys.

You couldn't join the Society Boys. You couldn't be hazed into it. There was no rush week. You had to be born into the exclusive circle.

The members came from old families, old money, and old power. They were the descendants of the Royalty our country had fought to free ourselves from. The grandsons of the tycoons of New York. The heirs of land barons of the west.

I'd known about the Society Boys my whole life. I'd watched the rotation of new and older boys coming and going. I'd seen the terrible things they did to each other, to those outside their circle. The competition and the undercutting. I'd seen the hazing they'd put gullible outsiders through, making them think they could one day join their exclusive Society.

They all lived in one house just outside of campus. It was massive, a mansion you had to buy into. The Boys threw parties that were unbelievable, because they had endless amounts of money. Their second largest one was this week, when they established their place at this school as the top dogs.

That was a part of the reason why it was so quiet in here tonight.

We'd never looked in each other's direction twice. I was the daughter of professors, and we would never be rich or powerful. I wasn't a stuck-up asshole, so they would never be my friends.

Maybe I was done with friends.

Do adults continue to make friends, unless it's at work?

I ignored the other students as I headed toward the far back reaches of the library, where the Latin volumes were. I was well familiar with the book we'd been assigned. I'd read it twice my sophomore year of high school. But it had been enough years that I didn't mind a refresher.

A set of double glass doors was pushed open in this room. It smelled of old paper—yellowed and aged—and smoke, even though fires were never permitted in that old fireplace anymore. Only two of the study rooms in the whole library still allowed them.

My eyes roved over the titles, well worn, some had entirely disappeared from the spines. I hadn't read them all, but I'd gone through at least a quarter of them. I had a goal to make it through them all by the time I took my own professorship here.

I stepped across the room and my eyes trailed down the shelf, searching for the assigned title. But they skipped from one to the next.

It wasn't here. Not a single copy.

I huffed a noise of annoyance.

I turned on my heel and walked out the doors. I weaved my way through the aisles, the few students, and cut down the farthest row, my eyes fixed on the desk.

I slowed as I approached it. I'd known the head librarian, Mrs. Walker, my entire life. She'd been a close friend of my mother's and they were close to the same age. She'd had assistants, changing every single year, students, working in exchange for scholarships.

But they were always, always women.

There was no one at the desk, except for one man, sorting through books in a way that told me he was in fact, working.

He wore slacks and a button up shirt. Most of the male students wore suits—Alderidge men certainly abided by the saying "dress to impress." The Society Boys made it a point to flaunt how much they had spent on their suits and ties and shoes.

I could tell this man wasn't wealthy. The clothes were basic. But they were exceptionally well cared for.

His hair was somewhere between blond and brown, depending on how the light hit it. It was neatly parted and combed.

I studied his face as he looked down at the books and continued his work. There was something slightly hollow, maybe even gaunt about it. His eyes looked tired, his cheekbones told me he didn't eat enough. He was tall and lean, and as I watched him sort through the tomes, I noted his long fingers.

There was something elegant about him, but also a little bit savage and feral. His hands were covered in scars.

I realized suddenly that those long fingers had stopped moving.

My eyes slid up, and his were locked on me.

He'd caught me staring.

"May I help you?" he asked.

His voice was lower than I expected. His words were also quiet. His voice was the kind that sent vibrations right down into the center of your chest and left you wondering how it ever had the power to make it all the way there.

"You work here." I said it more as a statement than a question, because I knew the answer, but the words slipped out before I could reason with my brain and my lips.

The look in his green eyes darkened slightly. "And here the world claims to be so progressive," he says. "Civil Rights are moving forward by leaps and bounds, women are going to get NASA to the moon, yet the whole of Alderidge gapes at the male librarian assistant."

"No," I said, my words jumping out too loud and quick. "It's not like that, I think it's actually great. I just…I've lived here my whole life, recognize a pretty good chunk of the students, but you don't look familiar. I didn't realize Mrs. Walker was taking freshman assistants."

He closed the book that had been lying open, his eyes and hands returning to the books. "This is my third year at Alderidge. I'm a junior."

"Oh," I said, my lips closing in surprise. "I…I'm sorry. I don't know how I've missed you."

"You're not the only one," he said, looking back at me briefly. His gaze very quickly shifted up and down. "But you're not wrong. I prefer to stay in the background."

I wasn't sure what to make of his statement. Now that I'd seen him, I wasn't sure how I could have ever missed him. One, for his height. He was lean, which made him seem taller than he really was. And two, in just the way he looked. There was something a little… dangerous about his appearance. Like he had nothing to prove, but everything to lose, from his pressed slacks to his hair.

"I'm Margot Bell," I said, extending my hand. I watched as his eyes looked at it. Two seconds passed, and I felt my heartbeat quicken, though I didn't know why.

Finally, he took my hand, shaking it twice. "Nathaniel Nightingale."

Even his name was a little intimidating and elegant.

"It's nice to meet you, Nathaniel," I said. "Do people call you Nate?"

"No," he answered simply.

He was a little cold and a lot blunt. I wasn't quite sure how to take it yet.

"I'm hoping that maybe someone's checked a book back in," I said, moving on. I rattled the title off to him and he turned to check the large rolling shelf behind him, filled with books waiting to be returned to their proper places.

My eyes dropped to the desk. There were dozens of books spread across the counter. Some of the titles were familiar, some weren't. Some I'd heard of, some were materials for classes far above my own freshman courses.

A particularly old-looking book lay just to my right. It was opened to the middle, like maybe Nathaniel had been reading before he'd gotten busy working.

I braced my forearms on the counter and leaned forward, curious about what someone like him might read for enjoyment, or perhaps what he was studying for his degree.

The words were in a language I didn't recognize, though many of the characters were of Latin origins. I squinted, tilting my head, trying to decipher it since it was upside down.

I glanced up, seeing that Nathaniel's back was still turned to me as he searched for my book. Quickly, I reached across the counter and dragged his toward me.

I felt stupid for not being able to read it upside down. As soon as I pulled it toward me and turned it right side up, I could read every single word.

My eyes took in a few key words while I looked at the top for a title or an author or a subject.

Soul.

Feeling.

Origins.

A hand with long fingers slapped down in the middle of the spine, and I cringed when it made a cracking sound. With wide, startled eyes, I looked up to meet Nathaniel's.

"This book is very old, and from my personal collection," he said, his voice dark and hinting at controlled anger. "It is not for student study."

"I wasn't—" I started to defend. But I absolutely was.

With his long fingers, he dragged the book toward him and away from me, out of my grip.

As my eyes fell back down to it, the words once more looked foreign.

"Wait, I…" Words left my brain as I tried to pick out the words I'd read before. But like the first moment I looked at it, they were once more foreign. "What… what language is that written in?"

"Scottish Gaelic," Nathaniel said, sliding it back to the place I'd found it, and closing the cover.

I blinked, shaking my head. "I don't know much Gaelic, but I swear I could read that page for a second."

Instantly, Nathaniel's gaze snapped back to me, his brows furrowing with his penetrating gaze. "Are you a Celtic languages major?"

I shook my head. "No, Latin."

I didn't know what to say as Nathaniel continued to stare at me, his gaze intense and intimidating.

He took half a step back from the counter and bent. I watched in confusion as he rummaged around for something below, where I could not see. Eight seconds later, he stood back up, and laid the book I had been looking for on the desk.

"This is also from my personal collection," he said, his voice calmer now, but more controlled sounding. "The library currently doesn't have any more copies. I'll need it back. But you can borrow it for the weekend."

My eyes slid back up to his and I just looked at him for a few seconds too long, feeling totally at a loss for words. But eventually, I blinked, and nodded. "Thank you," I said, cautiously reaching for the book and pulling it toward me.

He just held my gaze, and I couldn't help feeling like he was studying me. Like he was trying to read some kind of information right off my skin.

I couldn't take the stare-off any longer. I looked away, tucking the book back into my bag. "Do you work again Monday evening?" I asked, trying to move past the intensity.

"Yes," he replied simply. As if the word snapped him back into the reality of this moment, he turned, and continued working his way through the books, and I felt the finality of our conversation.

I hadn't realized how shallowly I'd been breathing until I turned and walked down the aisle of study desks, and finally took one deep breath.

CHAPTER TWO

Sunday evening played out much the same as all the others in my life.

Dad and I had eaten dinner and cleaned up. We'd washed the dishes together, dried them, put them back in the cupboard. Then we made our way into the living room. From mid-September to May there would be a fire roaring, but we weren't quite there yet, so for now, Dad had lit half a dozen candles and set them on the hearth. Together, we each sat in an overstuffed chair in the bay window, and we read.

I doubted anyone in the world had read more than my dad. He went through a book a day, rarely did it take him two to finish one. He read everything, from autobiographies to science-fiction, and from books on physics to research papers on the dark arts in ancient times. He devoured it all.

I guessed that's what made him such a good professor. He was interesting and he was smart.

I was nearly done with the book Nathaniel had lent me. The refresher had been good, though not entirely necessary. I'd remembered more than I expected and completed the homework assignment without any trouble. Now I just wanted to finish the book again for my own fun.

The scent of the house was warm and cozy. Our house smelled like a library, because it very nearly was one. Every spare wall in the house contained a bookshelf. None of them matched. But every single shelf was stuffed to the brim. It was a hobby of my parents, to rummage books at yard sales and used bookstores. Occasionally the area libraries would sell their surplus books, and you could guarantee my parents would be there.

Where there weren't bookshelves, the floors creaked, and the house tilted to the north just a little bit. It was old. One of the oldest in Harrington, built along the perimeter around Alderidge. All the houses on this row belonged to professors. They were all a mix of brick and white siding, dating back over two hundred years. When Dad wasn't reading, or teaching, or grading papers, he was fixing problems on the house, or hiring someone to do the job.

But this was home. And it had been home my entire life.

I came to the end of the book, filled with that familiar sensation of reflection and sadness that the story was over. I closed it and uncurled my legs from beneath me.

"I'm heading to bed," I said softly. I stood and stepped forward to press a kiss to my father's forehead. He glanced up at me quickly with a smile, whispered goodnight, and returned to his book.

The stairs creaked as I climbed them. The handrail was getting worn down from being touched so much. We would need to get it re-stained and lacquered again soon or there would be splinters to deal with.

I started down the hall and passed my parents' bedroom with a quick glance.

The bed was perfectly made. My father's nightstand was, of course, filled with books, but also random coins, the occasional tie, and a pocket watch he was always forgetting.

My mother's side contained an array of books and a few scraps of paper with her loopy handwriting. All of it was covered in a thick layer of dust.

Her slippers lay beside the bed, unmoved in a long time.

While my father's side of the room was well used, lived in, my mother's was frozen in time.

I tore my eyes away from their bedroom and moved down the hall.

I brushed my teeth in my small bathroom with the clawfoot tub. I braided my hair over my shoulder and turned out the light.

There was a small dormer in my bedroom with a window that looked out at the side of Alderidge. My room, just like the rest of the house, was filled with books. Not posters of singers. There weren't clothes strewn everywhere or rows of shoes taking up entire walls.

I climbed into bed, pulling the blankets up to my chin. I laid Nathaniel's book on the nightstand, feeling uneasy and excited at the same time about seeing him again tomorrow evening.

I TURNED in my paper in my Latin class and listened intently to the lesson, even though I knew everything Laurence talked about. When the class was over, I wrote down the next assignment in my planner and packed up my things.

I walked out of my classroom and turned left down the hall to head to my next. I was halfway there when I spotted my father standing in the doorway to his classroom, talking with Nathaniel. My father's expression was relaxed, casual, none of what I felt during my one and only conversation with the strange young man. Nathaniel listened to my father with rapt attention, his hands in the pockets of his slacks.

I really wanted to go over there and see what they were talking about. It was likely nothing. There was a high probability that my father was his professor or had been in a past semester.

But I didn't have time right now. I had to get to my writing class, and it was on the opposite end of this building.

The lesson today was dull, and I had to use every ounce of my willpower to concentrate. This was one of those classes that started off with rudimentary basics. This was all stuff that should have easily been mastered by everyone in high school.

Which likely meant that we were about to launch forward with rocket speed at any moment. This was Alderidge, after all.

I walked out of class, ignoring my growling stomach. My schedule had worked out in a way that I started early in the day, ran through the lunch hour, and I finished by 1:30. It was going to take a few weeks for my stomach to adjust to eating lunch that late.

I'd just turned down the hall to head to my Social

Studies class when I suddenly found myself shoulder-to-shoulder with Nathaniel Nightingale.

We looked at each other in slight surprise at the timing but fixed our sights forward.

"When you told me your name was Margot Bell and you knew most of the other students here, I did not put two and two together that you are Professor Bell's daughter."

"Guilty," I said as we walked through the halls side by side.

"Your father is a brilliant man," Nathaniel said. "I've taken two classes from him."

"So, you're a history major?" I asked, aware of how close he suddenly was as the crowd surged, pressing us together.

"I am," he confirmed. "With a minor in linguistics."

"Which explains how you were reading a book written in Gaelic."

I felt his eyes flick to me, weight and evaluation in his gaze. He was studying me, my features. "Yes," he said after a beat too long, which made me think it was a lie. But he didn't look away, which was…confusing. "I also speak French and have studied Olde English. I'm currently working on German and Italian."

"You don't need to brag, Nathaniel," I said. "You've

already been admitted to Alderidge. I figured out you were smart without so many words."

I looked back at him and his brows furrowed for a moment. "I thought I was merely making conversation, Miss Bell."

I gave a little shrug and barely contained a smile. This was fun. I hadn't had someone my own age to harass in a while.

The problem was that I didn't think Nathaniel realized I was just making conversation, too.

I eyed the door to my class and Nathaniel slowed when I did, pausing outside the door. "Well, perhaps I can teach you Latin as well, and then you'll be the smartest lad in all the land."

Nathaniel looked at me, and I could see the evaluation in his eyes. He didn't know me yet, didn't know how to have a conversation with me. I didn't know him yet either and I had no idea how much I could tease or joke.

"You teach me Latin, and I'll see if I can teach you to read that book," he said, and I knew he meant the Gaelic book I'd thought I could read at the reference desk.

"Deal," I said, and for a moment, my smile cracked through.

Nathaniel didn't smile though. He continued to

stare at me like I was some kind of puzzle. His eyes were dark, concentrated, slightly confused.

But I smiled and turned for my classroom. Just before I stepped inside, I turned back, my hand on the doorframe. "I'll see you in the library tonight at seven?"

This broke his darkness, and he blinked. Just once, he nodded. "I'll see you at seven."

I let myself smile once again and turned into my class.

Nathaniel Nightingale was a strange one. He was so serious, so focused. I didn't think he was flirting with me, but he stared more intently than any of the three boys who had ever asked me out. He was direct, yet mysterious.

Maybe I shouldn't have been so fascinated by him. He could be trouble. But I was finding it hard to look away.

I PUT the finishing touches on dinner and called Dad down to eat. Together, we sat at our little table.

"I saw you talking to Nathaniel Nightingale today," I said as we ate.

Instantly, a smile crossed my father's lips. "Brilliant boy. Do you know him?"

I gave a slight shrug. "I met him at the library the other day."

"That doesn't surprise me," Dad said. "He was always my best student."

"He wasn't necessarily studying," I said, picking at my chicken. "He was working. I didn't mean to make him feel bad about being a male librarian, but I think I might have embarrassed him."

"I highly doubt that," my dad said, shaking his head. "He was a student of mine both his freshman and sophomore year. I've watched that young man endure a lot from the Society Boys. I don't think much of anything bothers him."

I mulled that over, not quite sure what to think of it. Maybe that explained some of the darkness that hovered in his eyes. "What else do you know about him?" I asked.

Dad swallowed his bite and shrugged. "Not that much, really. Just that he's a history major and has an incredible memory. Bit of a loner. He's at Alderidge on scholarship."

This impressed me. Alderidge didn't give out many scholarships. I was on one, but that was because I had two parents who were professors here. For Nathanial to obtain a scholarship, he must have had a truly brilliant mind.

"What were you two talking about today?" I asked.

My father's eyes rose up to meet mine. His chewing

slowed. "Why the sudden interest in Nathaniel Nightingale, Margot?"

I considered for a moment. I've never talked to my dad about boys much, even though he was the only option in the years I was allowed to date. I've only ever had one boyfriend, and that had only lasted for three months.

But I always liked to be honest with my father.

"I had kind of a weird interaction with him at the library," I said. "Not bad, but…he's just a little odd. He lent me the book I needed for Laurence's class, from his personal collection. I'm taking it back to him tonight."

My father looked at me for a few long moments, evaluating the situation. I trusted him. If there was anything to be worried or alarmed about, my father would tell me. If he'd gotten any negative impressions from Nathaniel, my father would warn me.

"Not all boys are social and smooth like the Society Boys," he finally said. "And that's a good thing."

I held his eyes for a few more moments, trusting him and my own gut.

I finished my meal. I grabbed my bag, including Nathaniel's book, and I headed for the library.

CHAPTER THREE

Tonight, the library was busy. At least half of the tables in the study area were filled.

At the table in the very middle, were the Society Boys.

They weren't hard to pick out. It was almost as if they were clones of the same person. Well cut, slicked back hair. Fancy, pressed suits. The shiniest shoes. Expensive overcoats. Mean eyes. Watching, probing stares.

They were like a club that didn't really do anything but stick together on campus, meet once a month for a party, live in the same houses on campus, and make life harder for the outsiders.

There was their leader—David Sinclair. Devilishly handsome, filthy wealthy, and a complete and utter asshole. And his right-hand man—Borden Stewart, the literal descendant of Scottish Royalty. His family was one of the oldest in the States and made short time in amassing a cache of wealth and property.

All of their other head boys were just as pretentious and unbearable. James Richards, Donald Kline, Gerald Paulson, and Howard Starrling.

I purposefully avoided the table the Society Boys sat at, skirting around the far side and walking down the aisle. But when I got to the circulation desk, I didn't find Nathaniel, only Mrs. Walker.

"Evening, Margot," she greeted me with a warm smile and a wink, because she always winked. "How's your first week of university been?"

"Good," I said to her, flashing her a smile. Once upon a time, she and my mother had been close friends. But time can change anything. And now Mrs. Walker was just the friendly woman who ran the library. "Not too big of a deal yet. Though I'd guess it will start getting a lot more intense this week."

"I haven't worried about you at school for one second," she said, winking again.

I offered her a smile, pushing back a whole lifetime of memories of her in our kitchen on weekends, laughing and making jokes with my parents. "Hey, I was supposed to meet Nathaniel Nightingale. Do you know where I might find him?"

Mrs. Walker tipped her chin up in the direction over my left shoulder. "He took some books to put back in the British Isles section."

"Thanks," I offered with a forced smile.

I set off through the rows of books. Past the fiction section. Past the rooms of Greek and Roman history. I aimed for the fourth room down, my heart starting to beat a little harder, a little faster.

As I stepped into view of the room and found his back turned to me, I paused for just a moment.

What was it about Nathaniel Nightingale that set me so on edge, yet fascinated me so much?

I cleared my throat and he whipped around instantly, fixing his furrowed brows on me. When he saw it was only me, he turned back to the cart of books and continued putting them away.

"I was not intending to brag earlier," he said with his back turned to me.

A smile pulled at my lips and I felt a little embarrassed over the fact that my heart did a little flutter, knowing he'd been thinking about our conversation all day. "I knew you weren't bragging. I was just teasing you."

He looked over his shoulder at me as he put several books back on the shelf. I couldn't quite read his expression. I would need to get to know him a lot better before I could understand the guarded looks in his eyes.

When he didn't say anything, I pulled his book from my bag. "I brought your book back. Thank you for letting me borrow it. I feel pretty confident about my paper."

"You seem pretty confident about everything when it comes to Alderidge," Nathaniel responded as he turned and took the book from my extended hands. "Except maybe me."

I blinked. He was so direct. Not many people were that way. People guard their feelings, they talk in circles, they play games.

"I can't quite get a read on you," I say, being honest in return. "It's throwing me off."

For the first time ever, a little smile crooked in one corner of his mouth.

He set his book down on the cart and turned back to the task at hand. He took four more books and scanned the shelves to find their proper place.

"The surname Bell derives from Middle English," he said, and once more, I was intrigued by just the sound of his voice. Even his way of speaking was unique. His low tone, the quiet timbre of his words. "It can come from multiple countries around Europe. Scotland, England, France, Norway, Germany. Do you know your family history, Margot?"

I blinked. Nathaniel couldn't be more than twenty-one years old, maybe twenty-two if I was stretching. And there he was, talking about history outside of a classroom, asking about ancestry.

"My great-grandfather came from England to America when he was pretty young," I answered. I crossed the room and took a seat in the leather chair beside the empty fireplace. "He came with his younger siblings, but I know a lot of the older siblings stayed behind in England."

Nathaniel gave no indication that he'd heard me, but I knew he had. He was quiet for a long moment, and I could nearly feel the gears turning in his head. Though I didn't know why. I would bet nearly a quarter of this country had origins tracing back to England.

"And what about your mother?" Nathaniel asked after a moment that dragged on too long for comfort. "What is her maiden name?"

My throat tightened instantly. There was a bad taste in the back of my throat and my palms instantly felt slick with sweat.

"McGregor," I answered, even though I didn't want to share the information with him. I truly didn't want to talk about her with a stranger. "Amelia McGregor Bell."

"Scottish," Nathaniel said simply, and in a way like

it explained something. I was grateful that he didn't ask anything more or say anything else about it.

"The name Nightingale is also English," he moved on. "It originated as a nickname for someone who could sing well. I guess some things die out over the centuries."

My eyes slid back up to him, but he kept his back turned to me. A little smile curled the corner of my mouth.

I think Nathaniel just cracked a little bit of a joke.

"I've been attempting to compile my family history for the last few years, but it's proven to be exceptionally difficult."

"Why is that?" I asked.

He put the last book on the shelf and stood there, looking at the spines. "Because my parents were drug addicts, which landed me in state custody when I was three years old. I've been unsuccessful in even learning their parents' names."

I sat back in my seat, shocked at his very honest and personal confession.

Nathaniel turned around and walked to the seat opposite of mine. He sank down into it, and I was surprised when he slouched down, crossing one ankle over the opposite knee. He'd always been so composed and proper, seeing him like this was startling.

"I'm really sorry to hear that," I said, at a bit of a loss for words.

He simply gave a shrug, his eyes drifting over to the fireplace. "It's a privilege most don't see," he continued. "To know one's origins. We find such interesting stories in our own personal histories."

I didn't even realize he'd done it, but he'd put me in an open state of mind, just by sharing three sentences of his own vulnerable past.

"I had a great-grandmother who was hung in Salem because they thought she was a witch," I blurted in a low voice.

Nathaniel's eyes flicked back to meet mine.

"On my mother's side," I continued. "She and her husband had only been living in Salem for just over a year, with their three little ones. They put her on trial with the others. Declared her a witch and hung her. Her husband's journal said they did it right in front of their children."

I saw the gears turning in Nathaniel's eyes once again. His right hand was balled into a fist, supporting his head which was leaned against it, but his left hand tapped his thigh sporadically.

"1693 then. Fascinating," Nathaniel said, his words slightly breathy. "And absolutely tragic."

I was impressed with his ability to recall years and

history instantly. I had no doubt in what my dad said about Nathaniel being his best student.

I was about to open my mouth when someone stepped into the room.

A young woman about my age startled when she saw us. She placed a hand over her heart and shook her head, though she must have decided she needed something more than she felt awkward for interrupting our conversation, because she stepped inside and started browsing the titles.

I didn't know what else to say. Truly I didn't.

So I stood, slinging my bag over my shoulder.

"Thank you again for letting me borrow the book," I said, stepping toward the door. If Nathaniel was surprised or bothered by my quick decision to leave, he didn't show it. "I'll…I'll see you around."

"Goodnight, Margot," he said, his voice ever cool and even.

I turned and left the room.

CHAPTER FOUR

On Wednesday, I stepped out of my Social Studies class, thinking it might be nice to go down to the beach since the weather was still nice. But when I walked out, I found Nathaniel leaning against the wall across from the door. There was no question he was waiting for me.

"Hi," I said, the word coming out awkwardly while I tried to sort out what this meant.

"Hello," he answered. There was something lighter in his expression today. "I…I wondered if you were free this afternoon. I don't work at the library on Wednesdays and Thursdays."

I felt my face blush, which was embarrassing. And a little smile started pulling on my lips.

But still, I nodded.

"I…I was actually thinking of going to the beach today," I said as we started down the hallway. "The weather is supposed to be nice for a few more weeks. I thought I'd soak up as much sun while I could."

Looking at Nathaniel, he didn't look the type to soak up as much sun as he could, but he nodded his head in agreement anyway.

"I need to run home and drop off my books, and change," I said, my eyes focusing on the doors in front of me, the ones that would lead to my house. "Do you live close enough to campus that you could go get changed?"

Nathaniel nodded.

"I'll meet you at the archway in twenty minutes?" I didn't mean to form it as a question, but Nathaniel seemed so out of sorts, I didn't want to scare him off.

He only nodded once more. I gave him a little wave, smiling to myself as I headed down the hall at a quicker pace.

Twenty-two minutes later, I walked across the well-manicured lawn of Alderidge toward the archway that faced the ocean and led down to a stone pathway to the beach, a bag with a wadded-up blanket over my arm. I wore a white sun dress. I rarely wore it, because I felt like I was trying too hard to be something I wasn't, some sunny beach girl from California. But secretly, I loved it and wished I could wear it more. I'd also donned a floppy hat.

Nathaniel was already waiting at the arch. I took him in as I approached and realized he almost looked like an entirely different person outside than he did within the dim walls of the school. He seemed thicker, not quite as wiry. His hair was lighter. His skin was darker than I expected.

He didn't look as comfortable out here in daylight as he did within the walls of the library.

He turned when he heard my approach, and I didn't really mind when I watched his eyes run up and down me.

"You look like an entirely different creature out in the sun, Miss Bell," he said as I came to stand in front of him.

"Funny, I was thinking the exact same thing about you," I said.

I'd never forget it, the first time he smiled then. It wasn't big. It was still controlled. But he smiled, showing me a hint of white teeth and an annoyingly adorable dimple on either side of his mouth.

"Her bite is still the same, though."

There was something light that shone in his eyes as he looked down at me. And I thought then that maybe he should get outside of the school's walls more often.

"Shall we?" I asked.

Nathaniel turned to face the ocean and extended his arm, his elbow crooked out. I smirked at him, and he didn't miss it, but I took it anyway, and let him take the bag in my hand.

We made our way down those steps and then stepped out onto the sandy beach. We pointed south, wandering instead of finding some place to lay the blanket down and gaze out at the water.

"So, you have one more year at Alderidge after this," I said, looking over at Nathaniel. "That would make you…twenty-one?"

He nodded. "I'll be twenty-two come the end of November. And how about you, Margot?"

"I'm still eighteen," I answered, hating the answer. I'd resented the attachment of teen to my age since I was sixteen. "But I'll be nineteen the second week of September."

"You say both your parents are professors," he continued. "You're a Latin major. Does that mean you plan to become a professor as well?"

I shrugged. "I guess it's the family legacy. My parents have both loved their jobs. My whole life has been at Alderidge. It wouldn't be so bad to take a job here."

Nathaniel looked over at me, studying my face. "You mean that, don't you?"

I looked out at the sea. "I might not be the best at

making friends my own age, so I guess you could say some aspects of my childhood were lonely. But yes. I've loved it here at the University. This town. All of it. It's home. I'd be happy being a professor, like my parents."

We'd walked past the university's property. Now there were a few homes. Up ahead there was a restaurant.

I looked over at Nathaniel. "What about you? Two years of university left. What's the plan after that?"

Nathaniel looked straight ahead, walking along our path. I didn't think he liked the sand getting in his shoes very much. "I'd like to maybe travel around the world, further studying all the sites I've been fascinated by my entire life. And then I think I'd like to teach, too. Maybe not here at Alderidge, but somewhere."

I looked up at him, studying his face while he watched where we walked. "I thought I was the only one in our age range," he looked down at me then, "that was bad at making friends. You're pretty good at staying invisible, Nathaniel. But I see you now."

The intensity in his eyes was becoming familiar, and I saw it growing there now.

There was a house up ahead. Everyone in Harrington was familiar with it. It was a mansion, owned by a rich family in town. Beautiful and complex and sprawling, it had once been the nicest home in Harrington.

But a storm had rolled up the Eastern shore and done damage to a number of buildings, including Asteria House, named after the wealthy family who built it. They'd never repaired it. Only moved out and moved on, leaving it abandoned and decaying.

Nathaniel turned us up the slight bank, helping me up into the long grass. He led me toward the house. Together, we braved the steps leading up onto the massive back patio that spanned the length of the entire house. The boards creaked under our feet, but they held.

As if he'd done this before, Nathaniel pushed a door, and it swung open with a loud screech.

The inside was filled with wood paneling and floors and beams. It would have been beautiful at one point. We entered into what seemed to be a bedroom. An old four poster bed was pushed up against one wall, but the mattress was long gone.

I followed him through a door, and we walked out into a great room.

The floors were stained with water, and the once white wallpaper was turning green from mildew. I thought there might have once been a great chandelier hanging from the ceiling, but it seemed it had been looted out.

The house would be spectacular if only someone cared to fix it up.

"It's not the easiest, to make friends, or really any connections, when you're moved from house to house as a child," Nathaniel said.

"You said you were three when you were taken from your parents," I said. We wandered to a sitting room that overlooked the ocean. There were three chairs there, starting to rot away, but solid enough to support our weight. "Have you seen them since?"

Nathaniel settled into one of the chairs, looking out at the ocean through the windows. "They attempted to trick the courts into granting them custody again for a year. I remember being there once. Can recall their faces, or at least my child impression of them. But they disappeared after that. Then it was only foster families and group homes."

"Did you have any siblings?" I asked, my throat tight.

Nathaniel nodded. "I'm told I had an older brother and sister. But I don't remember them at all. We were all separated when we were taken away. I don't have any idea where they live now."

"I'm really sorry to hear all of that," I said. My heart ached for him. He didn't have parents. He had no one to go back to on Sunday nights for dinners. He didn't have a mom to take care of him when he was sick. A father to give him life advice.

Nathaniel's eyes slid back to mine. He didn't say

anything for a long moment, and I wondered what he was thinking.

"Your father is a good man," he said. "You're lucky to have him."

My throat tightened further, and I let my eyes drop down into my lap. "I know."

"But what happened to your mother, Margot?"

I knew the question was coming before the words ever left his lips. A piece of ice dropped into my stomach and my fingers instantly felt numb.

I hadn't talked about her in a long time. I hadn't even spoken her name in at least six months.

But maybe talking about the hard things would help. Maybe it was time I dealt with all of my feelings when it came to her.

"She simply disappeared," I said, the words coming out low and hoarse. I swallowed once, and slowly, my eyes rose back to meet Nathaniel's. I sat in the old chair with my forearms braced on my knees, slowly turning my hat in my hands.

"She was the very first female professor at Alderidge," I said. "Even though the Dean had been hesitant to hire her, and really only hired her to seem progressive, she'd excelled. You would have loved her. She was a linguist, too."

Nathaniel gave no reactions as I revealed the truth

to him. He didn't act surprised or angry. He simply listened.

"She and my father were happy. I think they thought it was a game, trying to gross me out by kissing all the time or holding hands or cuddling." Something bit at the back of my eyes and I blinked a few times to keep tears from welling. "She loved her job, at least as much as she loved me. Our family was happy. And we always took little trips together. Up to Boston for the weekend, or out to New York. We had a really good life."

It was hard, remembering how it had been. How normal things had seemed and how it never once crossed my mind that it could change.

"But just days after I turned fifteen, she disappeared," I confessed the heart-wrenching truth.

Three beats passed. Four. I could only concentrate on breathing even and slow. Could only try to tell my hands not to shred my hat.

This wasn't easy to talk about, but now that the words were coming out, I wanted them *all* out of me.

"It was literally like she just vanished," I said. "She hadn't packed any clothes. She didn't take any toiletries. She didn't take any of her books. Not even any money." I shook my head, and now I couldn't help it. Tears welled in my eyes, and I knew they would be bloodshot. "The police…they thought my dad had done something to her."

My eyes fixed out over the ocean, but I wasn't seeing the sunny blue sky or the calm ocean.

I was seeing the police tearing apart our house, going through our car, ransacking my father's office. I was watching him through a glass window while they interrogated him at the station. I was answering their questions about my parent's relationship and if I'd ever been afraid for my mother or feared my father myself.

"They investigated him for nearly an entire month before they treated it like a disappearance," I said, the words barely more than a whisper. "I knew they were looking in the wrong direction, and every day they blamed my father was another day less likely that we'd ever find her."

I looked down at my hat. I'd picked at the edge of it, all the way around, fraying it.

"The worst part is not knowing," I said. "If I did something wrong, if Dad did something wrong. If she just got tired of her life and ran away. Or if…if someone took her. If it was violent and terrifying. I don't even know if she's alive."

My voice cracked and then trembled on the last sentence.

And just like I never would have anticipated my mother's disappearance, I never would have anticipated it when Nathaniel rose from his seat and crossed to me. He pulled me to my feet, and with more warmth than I ever would have anticipated, he wrapped his arms around me, pulling my cheek against his chest.

And...it felt...good. So good.

I let it all out in a breath. My dread and resentment toward my mother slipped out of my chest with toxic release.

I wrapped my arms around Nathaniel, holding on to him tight, as if he could somehow save me from my own fear and worry.

He wasn't as thin as he looked. Through his linen shirt, I could feel strong muscles. In his arms, wrapped around me, I could feel agility. In his hands, I could feel strength.

"Our pasts build us as people, brick by brick," he said. "The experiences are difficult. We might not want them. But they make us strong. I barely know you, Margot. But I can already tell there's more strength in you than most others."

I looked up at him, craning my neck. He was a good seven inches taller than me. "Funny, I could say the same thing about you."

I could see it, bit by bit, I was breaking through Nathaniel's tough exterior. His serious and stoic demeanor was a façade. A defense. And who could blame him? He'd been cast aside since he was a toddler, seen as a financial burden and a case file.

I didn't want everything in his life to be heavy and hard.

We all deserved happy and light memories.

I let a smile crack through on my lips. I grabbed his hand and reached for the bag with the blanket. "Come on," I said, tugging him back toward the door we'd come through. "Enough with the serious and sad past. It's a beautiful day and I meant what I'd said about spending it at the beach."

I loved that I could do it. Nathaniel let a little chuckle slip through, and I looked back to see a smile cracking on his face as I pulled him back outside.

I didn't let go of his hand as I pulled him down the questionable stairs and started racing out toward the ocean. Sand sprayed everywhere and a flock of seagulls took to the sky with loud outcries.

Nathaniel dug his heels in just five feet from the water.

I didn't stop, though. I dropped the bag and I let go of him, because I'd pushed him far enough. I raced straight out into the water on my own.

I gave a screech of elation and shock as the water came up to my calves, then my knees. The water soaked the bottom two inches of my white dress.

"It's so cold!" I screeched. I turned back to shore,

finding Nathaniel standing safely out of the ocean's reach.

"This is Massachusetts," Nathaniel said with a chuckle and the shake of his head. "Not California. Stay out there too long and you'll catch your death."

"You're no fun," I said, reaching a hand into the water and splashing in his direction. I didn't even get close and he easily stepped out of the danger zone.

But he smiled, and that was all I was going for.

I really was freezing, though. So, slowly, I walked back to shore. "I've never been to California," I said as I walked up to Nathaniel. "I've always wanted to go. Really, I'd love to see any of the West Coast."

"Are you trying to tell me that secretly you're one of those hippies who wear beads in their hair and sit around a fire singing songs?"

That's when I knew I'd really done it. Gotten in.

He was cracking jokes with me.

"And what's wrong with that?" I teased back, raising my chin just a little.

He gave me an incredulous look, but there was a mischievous smile playing on his lips. "You're a born and bred East Coaster. It's simply not in your blood, Miss Bell."

I laughed, shaking my head. As much as I might dream, I knew he was right. I might let go and play and enjoy the sunshine when I'm very nearly alone, but when it came down to it, I was indeed a New Englander.

"Well, well, if this isn't the surprise of the century."

I jumped at the voice from behind us and turned to see a group walking down the beach, wearing swimming trunks and sleeveless shirts.

The Society Boys and a flock of their girls.

"Nathaniel Nightingale with a real, live woman." David Sinclair walked up, a snake smile on his face. His boys stopped on either side of him, Borden Stewart, and James Richards. "You alright, dear? I wouldn't put it past this library gremlin to force a woman into his company against her will."

I looked over at Nathaniel, who stared at David like he could melt him into glass on the sand. But he said nothing.

I turned cold eyes back on David and stepped closer to Nathaniel. "Well, we were having quite the afternoon before you and your lackies showed up. Though I guess I should be grateful you showed up now instead of later. That would have been a little embarrassing. Things were about to get a little less clothed, if you know what I mean."

This got quite the reaction from the crowd. Several 'ohs!" and snickers. Other noises of disgust. But mostly shock.

To my intense pleasure, David just glared at the two of us, at an utter loss for words.

"Come on, Nathaniel," I said, taking his hand and handing him the bag. "We can do it inside today. Last time it took me forever to wash the sand out of everywhere."

Nathaniel still said nothing as I started pulling him back in the direction of Alderidge. He simply glared at David and Borden and James.

I hated that he didn't know how to speak up for himself against stupid bullies like the Society Boys.

So, I would do it for him.

Someone behind us made a coughing noise but worked in the word *whore*. The other girls giggled stupidly. I heard James whispering something to one of the others.

But I didn't look back at them. I looked up at Nathaniel, leaned into him for show, and kept walking down the beach.

"Don't you realize what you've just done?" Nathaniel said once we were well out of ear shot.

The cold tone of his voice pulled my eyes back to his and I looked up at him with furrowed brows.

"I just turned that around," I said. I didn't like the cold tone of his voice. "I just kept David Sinclair from trying to humiliate you."

Nathaniel pulled us to a stop and fixed hard eyes

on me. "You think I give a damn what they think about me? Those boys have been trying to make my life hell since my freshman year. I can handle the Boys." He leaned just slightly closer, and I saw something soften in his eyes. "But you've just given them a reason to put a target on your back, Margot. They won't just let this slide."

I pulled my hand out of his and took half a step back. I blinked three times, trying to gather my thoughts, trying to form my next words carefully. "I'm not some fragile little girl, Nathaniel. I can handle the Society Boys, too. I've been avoiding their cat calls and their leering stares since I was fifteen. I'm not afraid of them, either."

I took one step closer to Nathaniel again. "Today's been pretty wonderful," I said, my voice dropping low. "I'd made my decision, that I want you as my friend. But there is something you need to know about me. That I won't be pushed around. That I won't be afraid, of anyone. Not the Society Boys, and not you trying to tell me how to act. So, you think about that. And if you can handle it, come and find me, and I'll decide if I made the right decision."

I grabbed my bag out of his hand, turned, and walked back down the beach, alone.

CHAPTER FIVE

I didn't see Nathaniel for the next few days. And that was perfectly okay.

I wasn't mad. I wasn't. But I didn't need a man in my life who was going to coddle me and act as if I couldn't stand up for myself or make my own decisions.

I didn't think Nathaniel was that kind of man. But I was going to step one little toe in that direction if there was a chance that he was.

So, I focused on my classes. I got an A on my Latin paper. I completed my first writing assignment. I aced my first Social Studies test. I got well prepared for my first World Geography test. And I did my best in Physical Education.

Dad and I went out to dinner on Friday night and

got lobster. It was a once-a-year thing, we wouldn't do it again until next year.

I put Nathaniel out of my mind, and I went about my life.

I passed Borden Stewart in the hall once. I held my chin high, gave him a tiny bit of a coy smile, and walked along my way.

On Friday, I walked into the bathroom at the exact same time David Sinclair was walking into the men's room.

I met his eye, let the coldness seep into my stare, and I walked into the women's room.

If he was going to start rumors about me, about what happened on the beach, let him. I'd find a way to deal with it, with him.

But nothing was whispered. I'd heard nothing in the halls. There were no suspicious looks tossed my way.

So, I went on with my life, just like I did any other day.

My birthday was approaching on Sunday, and Dad and I made plans to go up to Boston. I wanted clam chowder and more than anything I just wanted to wander the city and go to the Boston Public Library.

As much as I loved Harrington, I really loved Boston. Not to live in. There was just a feeling there in our neighboring city. I loved the old churches and the brownstone homes, the cobbled streets of Beacon Hill.

But on Saturday, I set off toward the library. I'd finished my book this morning, an old love story between a pirate and a proper lady. It had ended tragically but I'd still loved it. I was in the mood for another love story.

As I crossed the lawn to the University doors, I heard my name called. Looking out toward the north end of the building, I saw Nathaniel.

He stood alone, his hands in his pockets. The sun was most of the way down, casting a brilliant golden sunset across the entire sky. It made him look ethereal. Like something from one of the books I was after tonight.

"Can I talk to you?" he asked, his tone open and vulnerable.

I stood there in the grass for a solid eight seconds, thinking and considering.

And in the end, I stepped toward him. I held his eyes as I approached, and bit by bit, I let my defenses loosen just a little bit. In his eyes I didn't see any signs of a war or a fight. No rebuking. Just openness.

"I'd like to show you something, if that's okay?" he asked when I was two steps away.

I just nodded.

He set off across the grass and I followed him without saying a word.

He pointed us toward the north end of the university, the end that had been damaged in the storm and the fire. The end that was being overgrown by trees and wild nature. We cut along a stone fence that ended the manicured, cared for lawn, and then Nathaniel pushed a creaky gate open, letting me inside.

Because Nathaniel did, I ignored the signs stapled to the gate. *Danger: Unstable Ground. Keep Out.*

We entered into a garden, or at least I thought it had been at one point. There were overgrown rose bushes everywhere. Brilliant red roses grew in every direction, but I wouldn't dare try to claim any of them. I could see the thorns without getting too close. There were rows of garden boxes, though most of them were overgrown with wild things now. There was a statue of a colonial general in one corner, covered in bird droppings, and another of a pilgrim family up against the building, overgrown by the roses.

I'd lived here my whole life and I'd never once considered coming to this area. There were always warning signs along the fence that blocked off this garden. And the area did look unstable. The damage to the building was apparent. But still, I followed Nathaniel down a cobblestone pathway that looked surprisingly well-traversed. Deeper into the garden we went, passing other statues, some with missing limbs or heads, past a water fountain that had moss growing in it.

And then the wild garden opened up, and it was tame and manicured. And to the left, there was a solarium, attached to the long forgotten north wing of the university.

Glass walls rose up from the well-tended bushes and then angled up, attaching to the stone walls of the university.

"Come inside," Nathaniel said, inclining his head toward a wooden door on the side of it.

I didn't realize it until then, but a smile filled with enchanted wonder had broken out on my face. I stepped forward, following him to the door.

We walked inside, and I actually covered my mouth with my hands to contain the glee that filled me.

The north end of the university had been destroyed once. It had been abandoned for a few decades.

But inside this solarium, it was well loved and beautiful.

The wood floors showed signs of the fire, scorched along the wall shared with the university. But they'd been sanded and polished, gleaming beautifully.

Along the back wall, there was a hand-built bookshelf, rising with the angle of the glass roof. And it was filled nearly three quarters full with different titles.

An old wood desk was set at an angle from it, an old school chair pushed underneath it. An old leather couch ran along the stone wall. There was a fireplace against one wall and through an open door, I could see a bathroom. Against the glass wall that was covered by the rose bushes, was a queen-sized bed with a random array of bedding and pillows.

"You live here," I said. I should have formed it as a question, but everything in this room of glass screamed Nathaniel Nightingale. I could even smell him, like leather and old books and sandalwood.

"I found it my freshman year," he said, looking around at his space as I gaped at it in bewildered amazement. "It took me that entire year to fix it up, make it livable. But no one has bothered me here in the years since."

I turned back to face him and knew my eyes were bright, my smile growing on my face. "I love it," I said with the shake of my head. "It's…it's really wonderful."

And I hadn't realized I'd missed it until it was there again, but Nathaniel smiled. This one was real. Relaxed. Genuine.

He shrugged and looked around once more. "It's home. The only one I've really had."

I stepped forward, running my fingers along the

arm of the tufted leather couch. It was well worn, but I could tell he'd taken care of it as best he could. I walked across the room to his table. It was probably a dining table, considering its size. But his school papers were spread across it, assignments nearly or entirely completed. There were two books laying open, one a history book, one in what I was fairly certain was French.

Next, I stepped up to the bookcase. Much like my father's habits, there was an array of different books there. Mostly history, which I wasn't surprised by. But there were also books about physics and chemistry. Science fiction and love stories.

"Have you read them all?" I asked, picking out the few titles that I'd read.

"Yes," he answered simply.

I smiled again and shook my head. Suddenly, I was jealous. Yes, I understood that Nathaniel didn't have a family, that he'd been truly alone his whole life in a way I could never understand. But he had this space and had made it one hundred percent him. He'd claimed it as his own. He was independent. He was becoming his own person and adult in a way I still felt years from.

"Thank you," I said, meeting his eyes again. "For sharing this with me."

He nodded and walked forward, his eyes fixed on the bookcase. I could tell he knew exactly what he was looking for, because he walked directly, reached for a particular book, and plucked it from the shelf. Briefly, I glanced at the title. It was a history of the state of Massachusetts.

"Did you know that while the Salem witch trials were the last and only here in America, that there is still official litigation against witchcraft in parts of the Middle East?" With those long fingers of his, Nathaniel opened the book and flipped a few pages. He opened to a section and handed me the book, pointing to a particular passage. My eyes scanned it, searching for what he wanted me to see.

It was a list of the names of the men and women who were killed at the Salem Witch trials. And there, almost to the bottom, was the name of Mare McGregor.

My blood chilled, seeing her name there, listed among the accused and executed. I knew her name. I knew her story, as much of it as had been recorded by her son, my great-something-grandfather, Collin. But it was always so stark, the reality that she'd been hung. Killed.

"The entire world has a history of witch hunts," Nathaniel said, turning to the bookshelf again. He grabbed another book, opening it to a section. "Egypt and Babylonia."

He took another book, opening it and laying it on his desk. "Across the Holy Roman Empire."

My heart rate picked up. Sweat broke out on my palms.

Still, Nathaniel grabbed another book and another. "Russia, India, and even Africa to this day."

I watched Nathaniel, who stood with his back to me. His shoulders were tight. His head was bent low. His words were growing lower with each one spoken.

Gingerly, almost reverently, he reached for another book. The red binding was worn, and there were no words left. Gently, he grabbed it, and he held it to his chest, his arms carefully wrapped around it.

"It is estimated at around 60,000 people were killed for being witches over the course of three hundred years, in western Europe and central Europe alone. Tens of thousands more in Asia, countless more in Africa. Miraculously, only nineteen here in America."

There was a deep sound rushing in my ears and it took me a moment to realize it was the sound of my own blood. There was a heavy feeling of anticipation and uncertainty in my gut.

Nathaniel turned back toward me, and in his eyes, I saw something big.

"I cannot confirm that I am a direct descendant, but there was a William Nightingale killed during the

Lancashire witch trials in England in 1612." His eyes were fixed on me, but I could tell, he wasn't seeing me. He had fallen into history, into ancestry. "There are thousands of stories of accusations and trials and deaths."

"Yes," I said, wanting to bring us back to a place that wasn't so dark. I wanted everything to go back to being light. "And they were the result of mass hysteria and superstition. They wanted something to blame for bad harvests and hard financial times. A lot of innocent people died."

Nathaniel's focus returned to me. Three seconds passed, and finally he gave a little nod, but it didn't seem like a complete act of agreement.

He stepped forward, and gingerly, he laid the book in his arms on the desk. I recognized it then as the one from the library, the first day we had met.

"You said you cannot read Gaelic," he said in a low voice. He opened the book and looked down at it, gazing at the words with wonder. "But maybe you should try again."

"Nathaniel, I-" I began to protest. But he looked up at me and begged me with his eyes.

So, I crossed to the desk to stand beside him. I looked down at the words, remembering the silly experience with it before, now weeks ago. I could recognize letters, as I'd concluded before, some of them were of Latin origin. But I couldn't read any of it.

"I haven't learned Gaelic in the last few weeks, Nathaniel," I said, looking over at him. He looked at my face intently, as if he were waiting for something spectacular to happen. "I still can't read it."

Gently, he reached for my hand, wrapping his fingers around my wrist. I didn't know what he was doing, but I decided I trusted him enough to humor him.

He brought my hand forward, and gently, he set my fingertips down on the edge of the pages.

It was as if I'd blinked, and it turned into a different book.

One moment it was in unreadable Gaelic. The next, it was in perfect English.

I blinked, leaning in closer to the book.

A simple matter of will and asking, levitation is one of the simplest forms of magic.

My eyes read the line without a second of hesitation or translation.

I ripped my hand back from the book and took half a step back.

Instantly, the book was once more in a language I could not read.

The room was utterly silent. So quiet it pushed in on my ears and the only sound was my own heartbeat.

I felt Nathaniel's eyes on me. I felt meaning filling

the air. I felt anticipation. But also, momentous confusion.

Cautiously, I reached my hand forward again. Filled with fear and wonder, I touched the edge of the pages.

In levitation, most users have certain affinities, whether they be metal, earth, wood, life forms, etc.

Because it was the scientific method of proving a hypothesis, I removed my hand one last time and the words became unreadable.

I touched the pages, and my eyes relaxed as the words became readable.

"You can read it, too."

I looked up at Nathaniel and startled when he stood there with his right hand held up, his fingers generally pointed at the ceiling. And floating around his fingertips there were three paper airplanes, swirling, dipping and rising through the air. And that air around his hand had this…shimmer. Almost as if glitter floated in the air. But I couldn't quite focus on it. And the air seemed more…golden.

"What kind of trick is this, Nathaniel?" I asked, my words hoarse and quiet.

I'd never seen this look in his eyes. They were filled with…excitement. And hope. He shook his head. "It's not a trick, Margot," he said. He waved his fingers, and the airplanes set off toward the opposite end of the solarium. Gently, they floated toward his bed, flying in a circle over it. They followed each other in a line, doing a flip in the air and then flying over to the couch, where they dipped down low, soaring beneath it, before they aimed back at Nathaniel. There, they swirled around his fingers once again before they gently floated down to the table and landed on the book. "It's in my blood. And I believe it's in yours, too."

I shook my head and took a step back. Carefully I surveyed the room for strings or wires. I didn't understand why he was doing this. What woman has ever appreciated a magician when it came to a potential relationship? But as I looked harder and harder, I couldn't figure out how he'd pulled that off.

"I'm sorry, Nathaniel," I said, shaking my head. "I'm not into magic. I thought we were going to have a real conversation about what we talked about on the beach, but if you're just going to woo me with tricks, then I'm going home."

I took one step toward the door, but Nathaniel grabbed a blank piece of paper from the desk and shoved it into my hands. "I am not claiming to be some cheap magician," he said through nearly clenched teeth. "This is not a show and I haven't spent years hiding under the covers practicing sleight of hand."

I met his eyes. I should have been scared. He was acting crazy. He was saying crazy things.

But I wasn't. And maybe it was my thundering heart. Maybe it was the ringing in my ears.

Or maybe it was that image of the book changing in my mind.

The words I'd read.

"This is not a gimmick, Margot," he said. His eyes fell to the paper. "Feel it yourself. It's just paper. No strings. No wires or tricks."

I turned it over, and I saw it for myself, that it was indeed just a piece of paper.

"Watch," he said. He brought up his hands beneath mine, encouraging me to hold it up to nearly eye level, the piece of paper balanced flat on my palms. He lowered his hands and then laced them behind his back.

He stared at the piece of paper, his gaze focused.

My eyes ripped back to it when I heard it crinkle.

My eyes grew wide as I watched it crease and fold, as if it were being manipulated by invisible hands. It changed shape before my eyes, lying in my hands. And I felt nothing. No trick wires. There was no way he could be touching it without me knowing.

My breathing got heavier and faster.

In a matter of seconds, I began to see a shape take form.

In fifteen seconds, it sat there, perfect and formed.

A paper crane.

I was about to breathe out a disbelieving curse, when I jumped hard as the wings of the paper crane extended, and it lifted off from my palms.

Gently, gracefully, it flapped its wings, and set flight throughout the solarium.

I looked back at Nathaniel. The air shimmered with that gleam I couldn't quite describe or capture with my eyes. His hand glowed faintly golden as he pointed and directed it around the space.

"I think you could do it too, Margot," Nathaniel said as he directed the crane back to me. My hand shook as I held it up, my palm flat. It settled back onto my hand and then was as still and innocent as any other paper crane in the world. "Because you can read the book, I think you can do it, too. I think you and I are the same."

"And what the hell is that supposed to be?" I asked with a shaking voice.

"I don't really know," Nathaniel said, his voice little more than a whisper. He took a step closer and closer, until he stood right in front of me. His eyes went to his paper crane. "I think we might be the descendants of those who were burned at the stake for having real magic. Witch, wizard, warlock, mage. I think that we're the blood left over of those who had abilities that got them killed."

Fear spiked in my blood, and I instantly recalled all

the numbers he'd just told me. The witch hunts. The innocent lives lost.

He was claiming that not all of them were so innocent.

"Close your eyes, Margot," Nathaniel said.

I didn't mean to do it, but I found my eyes closing.

"Feel the crane in your hand," he said. He was so close I could feel his breath on my cheek. I could feel the heat coming off of him. "Ask it to move. Will it in your mind."

This was crazy. Nathaniel was crazy.

Maybe I was dreaming. Maybe I'd fallen on my way to the library and hit my head. That was the only real, logical solution to what was happening.

But I did as he asked because I wasn't blind to what Nathaniel had just done. And there was this feeling in my chest, one that asked me to be open.

I felt the crane.

I asked it to lift.

I imagined it.

But I still felt it on my hand. When I opened my eyes, it still sat in my palm.

"It's okay," Nathaniel said with an encouraging nod. "Nothing happened the first time I tried it."

"You're telling me that book taught you how to do what you just did?" I asked, because I needed more information. I needed something more solid.

"You saw the words on the page, Margot," Nathaniel said. His tone was rising just a little, his words coming out faster, with excitement. "Just…try again. Please."

I pressed my lips together and let out a hard breath through my nose. I gave him a doubtful look. But I closed my eyes. And I concentrated.

This is crazy, this is crazy, the words ran through my head, over and over again.

But I reached out.

Lift.

Float.

Rise.

I was filled with doubt and maybe a little fear. But I put the words out, thought them as hard as I could.

Something tingled at the back of my neck. It penetrated into my brain. Filled my chest. Ran to my fingers.

I'd never felt anything that felt so good.

"Margot," Nathaniel's voice whispered soft and quiet, next to my ear.

My eyes fluttered open, and I was immediately disappointed to see that the paper crane still sat in my hand.

But as I looked up at Nathaniel, to tell him this was pointless, my eyes went to the glass walls.

Outside, rocks and overgrown weeds, and broken roses floated in the air.

The second I saw them, a sharp gasp stabbed into the back of my throat, and everything dropped to the ground.

A string of curse words slipped from Nathaniel's lips. His hands went to his hair and he started talking in a string of words that left his mouth so fast, I didn't catch a single one.

I stepped forward, my eyes fixed on a single rose that now lay on the ground. I pushed the door open and stepped outside.

With trembling hands, I picked it up.

And…I felt something.

A call. A voice. A connection.

I kept my eyes open this time.

Laying my hand flat, I looked at the rose, and I asked it to rise in the air.

There was that familiar tingle at the back of my brain. And it didn't even hesitate.

The rose floated up into the air.

"You're one of us, too," Nathaniel breathed in wonder. He stepped to my side and his eyes watched as I turned the rose over in the air. "I…I think…what the book said. About affinities. I can make paper do anything. You saw the airplanes and the crane. Margot,

I think yours is some kind of…earth maybe. Because the rocks, the weeds. The rose."

His words hit me, and I lost my concentration. The rose fell to the ground and a few of the outer pedals broke off.

I turned sharply on Nathaniel.

"Explain everything," I said, the most urgent words I'd ever spoken.

CHAPTER SIX

A smile pulled on Nathaniel's face, and if I'd been in my right mind, I might have taken a second to appreciate the very first entirely uninhibited one I'd ever seen on his face.

But everything in my world had just changed. So I turned, following Nathaniel back inside.

"Most students leave once summer arrives," Nathaniel said as he crossed the solarium and walked to the desk. He closed the red book that had shifted all my perceptions, and held it between his long fingers. "But I stayed here," he continued as he leaned against the desk. There was wild excitement in his eyes. "I didn't have anywhere else to return to and no one had bothered me here in the solarium. I spent most of my time in the library, reading everything I could get my hands on when I wasn't working."

I crossed to the leather couch and sank down onto it. I twisted back so I was facing Nathaniel, my elbow propped on the back of the couch, my cheek supported by my fist.

"I'd been going through some old books in the Gavin room," Nathaniel said, and with the words, his voice got lighter, airier. "It was obvious no one had bothered with them in maybe a decade. But with them, I found this book." He held it up and my eyes locked on the red spine. He flipped it open and stared down at the words on the page in bewilderment. "I didn't even realize what was happening at first. I was holding it, so from the moment I opened it, I could read every word. At first, I thought it was a work of fiction, some old fairy tale."

There was a coy smile on Nathaniel's lips as he looked up at me from beneath his lashes.

Something exciting and dangerous stirred in my chest.

"I set it aside and continued going through the other books," Nathaniel said, moving on. "They were all old Gaelic books, which explained why no one had bothered with them. So few people speak it, the school hasn't bothered with it too much. But as I finished going through the books, I went to put them away and was going to let Mrs. Walker know that this one was in the wrong section. But as I went to pick it up, I dropped it."

My heart hammered. I imagined it as clearly as if I were seeing it in front of me. Nathaniel in the library. Surrounded by endless books. And the discovery of something beyond what the eye can make sense of.

"It opened to the middle section of the book," Nathaniel said. He laid the book on the table and removed his hands from it. "And it was all in Gaelic. Which, no, I don't actually know."

I'd been right before. He had lied about it.

"I was certain about it being a language I didn't know, but I was also positive that I'd just read half a chapter and understood every single word."

It played across my vision like a movie. I knew exactly what he was talking about, because I'd just experienced it for myself.

"I touched it again, and I couldn't explain it, but instantly all the words changed, and I could understand all of them," Nathaniel said as he reached out and touched the book. "I did it again and again, testing it over and over. And it worked every single time. When I touched the book, I could read it. When I didn't touch it, I couldn't understand a word."

"How?" I asked. I shook my head. "It doesn't make

sense. The ink can't be rearranging itself on the page. It's just not physically possible."

With just my few words of engagement, the light in Nathaniel's eyes brightened. He dragged the chair at the desk around, facing me. He sat on it backward, the book clutched in his hands. "I've never been able to test it without another." His eyes rose up to meet mine, and I couldn't help but smile along with him, excitement coursing through my blood. I twisted and got on my knees, my forearms resting on the back of the couch.

Nathaniel opened the book, letting its spine rest on his hands.

He looked up at me, expectation in his eyes.

"Gaelic," I said. I shook my head. "I can't read any of it."

"Fascinating," Nathaniel said. He lifted the book to me and handed it off, letting it rest in my hands.

Instantly, the words changed, and I could read every single one. I looked up at Nathaniel, into his dark eyes.

He shook his head and let out a little breathy laugh. "Not a word."

"So, it's not physically changing the ink," I said. My heart was racing. I was excited. Intrigued. Massively and wildly confused. But this… This was every scholar's dream. "It has to be, somehow…"

"Revealing itself to people," Nathaniel filled in for

me. "Like there's some kind of…glamour over the words, protecting itself."

"But you think it only reveals itself to certain people?" I ask.

Nathaniel nodded with a smile. "I know it does," he said in a rush. "I've tested it with half a dozen others. No one could read it. All they saw was the Gaelic. And I even asked one of the professors who knows Gaelic. He said it's just utter nonsense. Just random words that mean absolutely nothing."

In awe, I looked back down at the words. *There are always limits to an individual's telekinetic abilities. Weight, practice, the individual's mental strength all play a factor.*

I could read every word as clear as day.

"This is why I work in the library, Margot," Nathaniel said. He sat back in the seat, folding one arm over the other over the back of the chair. "Yes, I love books, and yes, I need the money to survive. But if I found this book, hidden in a forgotten section of the library, what other books might I find within the walls of the library?"

"You think there are others in the library, like this one?" I asked, my eyes widening and flicking back up to Nathaniel's.

He shrugged and shook his head. "Maybe not. But there might be. The University has collected books from around the world, and people are always donating others. And we know there had to be some truth to the Salem Witch Trials. You're a descendant of someone hanged for being a witch. There had to be others. I had to come from one of them. So maybe more of them had books that could teach us…whatever it was they were killed for."

"You really think it's an inherited ability?" I asked. My mind was spinning, thinking of all the things I needed to learn, all the aspects with holes, which was pretty much everything.

"I think so," Nathaniel said. "We…we could test it. Though I don't think it's going to work. Because unless your father is also the descendant of a witch…a mage, I believe it came through your McGregor blood."

My face froze. I felt it. All of my insides went a little colder.

He was saying my mother, who had disappeared, seemingly into thin air, was the descendant of witches, who gave me…what? Abilities? Powers?

"We could test your father with the book." Nathaniel said the words because it was the scientific method. To test everything we could. But I could tell he sensed my unease, my instant defenses rising at the mention of my mother.

I knew we would have to. We had to. We needed to know.

So I nodded, knowing there would be no big rush.

"What about others?" I asked. I changed the subject, and when I met Nathaniel's eyes, I saw that he knew why I needed to. "I mean, my grandparents are dead, so there's the end of that blood line. But do you…do you think there are others out there, like…us?"

He let out a hard breath, turning his eyes to the glass walls. "I don't know. Logically yes, there should be. Because I believe your lineage traces back to Scotland, mine to England. I don't think all these witch hunts started completely with no basis in truth, knowing what we now do. So I think this roots back to all of those places I just told you about. So, yes, there should be others. But why does history have no accounts of magic, accusations, trials, since 1700?"

I looked back in my memory to what Nathaniel just said about the witch hunts. I thought through my own learning.

He wasn't wrong. I couldn't think of anything that sounded like more than superstition or fairy tales.

"You think they were all killed?" I asked. "That they went…extinct?"

Nathaniel shrugged his shoulders again and shook his head. "They can't have gone extinct," he said. His eyes slid back to me. "You and I are proof of that. But maybe magic was just…forgotten about? What if those who knew how to use it…things just got too dangerous. Or they were killed and were never able to teach their descendants. I think maybe it was just…lost."

It seemed impossible. But the history of man is long, and many things have been forgotten over the centuries. Things change. Traditions die out. Entire libraries of knowledge and history are lost.

I closed the book and looked at it with reverence.

"I'm sure you've read the entire thing?" I asked.

"I nearly have it memorized by now," Nathaniel answered.

I nodded. I was certain he did.

"It's not just about levitation," I said. "You didn't just make the airplanes or the crane float. You folded it without touching it. You moved it all around the room. It's about…telekinesis, isn't it?"

A smirk formed on Nathaniel's lips, and it did strange things to my lower stomach. "Well concluded, Margot."

My heart beat faster and faster.

More. What if there were *more* books out there that could teach us how to do more?

It seemed impossible, but what I'd just done with the rose was impossible, and then I'd just done it.

"Show me something else," I said, handing the book back to Nathaniel. "I…I need to see more. I need… I saw it with my eyes, I…felt it. But it doesn't seem real."

I'd seen Nathaniel smile more in the last hour than I had in the entire two weeks I'd known him. He pushed his chair back and stood. I climbed to my feet, folding my arms over my stomach, and watched as he turned around, facing the bookshelf. He stood there for a moment, considering.

And then he raised his hands up, his palms facing the bookcase.

I watched his eyes slide closed for a moment, and he took a steady breath in and let it out.

His eyes opened again.

And the books on the shelf moved.

They slid out off the shelves and then shifted left or right, up or down. It was like a beautiful dance of mechanics. Left and up. Down, down, and right. They rearranged and as I watched, I found the order to the chaos.

They slipped back onto the shelves once more, now perfectly rearranged in alphabetical order.

"That's incredible," I breathed out, a breathy laugh bubbling on my lips. "And what was their order before? Because I know a librarian can't just put them haphazardly on the shelves."

Another smile came to Nathaniel's lips. "They were in order of favoritism and the year I read them."

I smiled again, shaking my head.

"This is crazy," I said, smiling. "Everything. The fact that a couple of college students found this. Your story. That real…" I shook my head again, because it really, truly felt insane, the words coming out of my mouth, "magic was found in a dusty section of a library. What…what are we supposed to do with it now?"

Our eyes locked and something stirred in my chest at the look in his eyes. "I think it means we study, Margot," he said. There was excitement there. A little danger. There was adventure in them and maybe a tiny bit of fear. There was an invitation. "I think it means we look for the rest, because I know there has to be more like us. I think it means we do whatever we want with it. And I think that we should do it together."

That caged, wild creature in my chest was let free then. It fluttered out into the rest of my body, filling up every space, sending my fingertips tingling, my toes on fire, the back of my neck burning.

"Okay," I said, having no idea what the future would bring.

Hours passed by in an instant. By the time Nathaniel and I looked up and took a breath from pouring over the book, it was pitch-black outside. The clock hanging on the wall said it was nearly two AM.

"Shit," I breathed, scrambling to my feet. We had been laying on the floor, both touching the book so we could read. "My dad has got to be freaking out. I can't just not come home, not after everything he's been through."

"I'll walk you home," Nathaniel said, also climbing to his feet. He reached for a jacket hanging on a stand beside the door and draped it over my shoulders. I felt my face flush a little bit as I looked back at him and said thank you.

We stepped out into the dark, overgrown garden. The air was humid but the breeze blowing in from the ocean pushed the temperatures low. Our summer days were fading quick. A few stars peeked out from behind the clouds that had rolled in.

We made our way across the lawn of Alderidge in silence. I didn't know what was on his mind, but mine was filled with everything. Possibilities, impossibility, history, the future.

But we walked side by side, our shoulders brushing every so often. And I knew it then, without a doubt, nothing was ever going to be the same. Not my future. Not the next day. And not the relationship between Nathaniel and I.

We walked through the gate and down the short road that led right to my front door.

A light glowed in the front window and I could see the shape of my father's outline, his head bent, and I had no doubt he was reading a book.

I breathed out another curse.

I meant to say goodnight to Nathaniel then, but he walked right up the stairs with me, and everything about his body language told me he intended to come inside.

So, I twisted the door knob and pushed it open.

My father's head whipped up immediately and he got to his feet when I walked through. He sucked in a breath, I had no doubt to lay into me, when his eyes shifted to Nathaniel as he walked in after me.

"I am so sorry, Professor Bell," Nathaniel said without hesitating, but also without rushing. His voice was calm, composed. "Margot and I got to talking about books and we lost track of time. I apologize for worrying you. I never meant to keep her out so late."

My dad blinked, his mouth closing. He didn't know what to say.

I didn't know what to say.

Nathaniel had spoken so calm and sincerely. I couldn't have been mad at him, and I knew my dad wouldn't be able to either, especially considering Nathaniel was one of his very favorite students.

"I appreciate you making sure she got home safely," my father said, sliding his hands into his pockets. "I can't really get angry when my daughter was distracted by books and smart company. Just…be more attentive next time, maybe."

Nathaniel gave a nod of his head. "I will, Professor."

I looked back at Nathaniel and I knew my face was blushing slightly, which was going to give my father all the wrong impressions. But Nathaniel and I shared a secret now. A big one. A monumental one. I couldn't not.

So, I handed his jacket back to him.

"Goodnight," I said, locking eyes with him. And everything was there. All the weight, all the magic.

He nodded to me, as well. "Goodnight, Margot. Professor Bell."

My dad nodded to him again, giving a little thin-lipped smile as Nathaniel stepped back outside and pulled the door closed behind him.

"I guess this means you got over your weird encounter with Nathaniel Nightingale?" my dad asked after five beats of silence as we both listened to the sound of Nathaniel's retreating footsteps.

I couldn't help it. A little smile broke out on my lips and a chuckle bubbled over my lips. My eyes dropped to the worn wood floors for a moment. "It was just…a misunderstanding. We worked it out and are on the same page now."

"And by same page, do you mean spending hours 'talking about books?'" He actually made quotation marks in the air with his fingers.

I blushed, which wasn't going to help my case. "No, we were actually talking about books the entire time." I couldn't help but smile though. "But…there might be something agreeable about spending time with Nathaniel. I might want to spend more time with him."

There was a smirk on my father's lips. I wasn't surprised by it. We'd always been honest with each other. Open. He took a step forward and laid a hand on my shoulder. "If it were just about any other boy at Alderidge I might have a few more stern words here at two in the morning. But Nathaniel isn't every other boy."

I looked up into his eyes, and I saw that he meant it. He genuinely liked and trusted Nathaniel.

"So, all I will say is goodnight. And considering the late, or early hour, we might not get as early of a start on Boston. But it is past midnight, so," he leaned forward and pressed a kiss to my forehead, "happy birthday, Margot."

I smiled, realizing it really was my birthday now. I wrapped him in a quick hug, and then walked upstairs.

After brushing my teeth and changing into a nightgown, I lay back in bed. Through the dim moonlight that came in through the window, I looked over at my nightstand. There was a geode that lay there, with a few other random knickknacks. I'd gotten it on some trip, even though it wasn't native to the area.

I picked it up and turned it over in my hands.

I let it lay flat on my palm.

I closed my eyes for a moment. I took a steady breath in through my nose and let it out through my lips.

I asked it to rise.

I felt it lift.

I opened my eyes, and there it was, as real as the bed I lay on, as real as the wooden floors beneath it, the geode had risen up into the air six inches. It turned over in the air, easy and gentle.

There was that tingle at the back of my head. It reached out to every end of my body. I felt alive and light and awake.

With control, I let the geode sink back onto my palm. I turned it over, looking for trick wires, knowing there were none.

How fitting, that the last normal day of my life had fallen on the last day of being eighteen. Nineteen was to bring on a whole new life for me.

CHAPTER SEVEN

Neither my father nor I woke up until after eleven. We didn't make quick time of getting ready to depart, so we didn't make it to the car to head north until just after twelve.

But we made our way toward the city. My father sang Happy Birthday to me at least four times. I'd laughed and joked with him and we'd both smiled the entire time.

Finding parking in Boston wasn't easy, but we managed. We'd grabbed a quick bite to eat for lunch, and then we headed in the direction of all my favorite spots.

I had dreams of owning one of the brownstone homes in Back Bay someday. There was something fascinating and charming about the rows of homes, surrounded by trees and greenery. The bay was beautiful.

We strolled up Beacon Hill, ducking into several of the shops along Charles Street. When we found a row of hand-crafted leather-bound journals, my father had taken one glance at the look on my face and bought one, wishing me happy birthday.

We set off through the Boston Common, a park in the middle of the city. There were statues scattered throughout, highlighting the long history of this city. Several vendors had carts set up, and I smiled with thanks as my dad bought us both ice cream cones. We made our way to a bench, enjoying the beautiful sunshine that would soon disappear.

"Did you ever consider a position at Harvard?" I asked as I watched a group of young adults crossing the park, laughing and smiling. "Or MIT?"

My father crossed one ankle over the opposite knee. "While they're both impressive," he said, licking at a bead of ice cream that rolled down the cone, "I far more enjoyed the smaller atmosphere of Alderidge. And while I love Boston as much as you do, it's not the easiest city to raise a family in."

I supposed that could be true, but as I looked around, I saw a group of young boys practicing football. I saw two mothers pushing strollers, young babies in them.

You manage wherever you're comfortable.

"What about Salem?" I asked, altering the trajectory of our conversation. "We have family history there. Did you and Mom ever consider living there?"

I sensed it the second her name came out of my lips. The air around us changed. My father's back grew a little straighter.

"You really think she ever would have wanted to live in a town where her ancestor was killed for being a witch?" he asked. His voice was low, his words a little rough.

"Do you know what Mare was accused of doing?" I asked. My heart beat a little faster, talking about my family history, knowing that she was exactly what they killed her for.

Dad shrugged, and he seemed a little relieved to not be talking directly about my mother. "Who knows. There was a lot of hysteria going on at the time. Those young girls later admitted they made it all up. Poor Mare might have simply crossed someone's sight at the wrong time."

I gave a nod, even though I knew it wasn't true.

I wondered if there was an account anywhere that would tell me exactly what each person was accused of.

I wondered what Mare was capable of. What did she get caught doing?

"So," Dad asked, tossing the last of his cone into

his mouth and chewing. He did that all the time, talked with his mouth full, and it had always driven Mom crazy. "Where to next?"

I bit into my own cone, sweeping my eyes around the park, at the towering, old city that surrounded us.

"The library," I said, my heart instantly jumping with anticipation and excitement.

"The library it is, then," Dad declared.

THE BOSTON PUBLIC LIBRARY wasn't a simple building. On a quick walk-through of the building, you actually wouldn't see many books. Architecture and sculptures and murals, yes. You almost had to know where to find the books. There were many different rooms and sections to the library. Some of them were old, as you'd expect. But there were newer parts to the library, containing newer books.

I smiled every time I walked through the front doors. A big set of stairs rose up and overlooking them were two lions carved out of marble. It really was like the gateway to a different world.

I kept track of my father up until we got to the top of the stairs, where we picked our directions. He went one way, and I went another.

I'd worried about having to explain myself and why

I wanted to simply open and touch books, but he was gone in an instant.

And besides, I was going into Latin. My obsession with books was a given.

I made my way through to the sections I had in mind. I admired the architecture as I went, the paintings, the numerous sculptures.

I loved how old Boston was. I loved its history and its stories.

I couldn't imagine what it would be like to travel somewhere that had much older history. Boston was still a baby compared to some parts of the world. What would England reveal? Scotland? The Mesopotamian area?

I wanted to see them all, to learn their secrets.

The world's secrets were much bigger than I'd ever anticipated, I'd just learned.

I went to the Gaelic section, hoping that I might have some luck with my own ancestors once again. With an employee keeping a watchful eye on me and everyone else in this room, I started at the beginning. One at a time, I pulled out a title. I opened it to the middle, set it on the shelf, and watched to see if the words changed.

A dozen books. Fifty. One hundred. Book by book, I looked through them, waiting to see if the words changed or made sense.

And then a sinking realization hit my stomach.

What if not every book that had something to teach Nathaniel and I was glamoured or hidden? What if they simply contained words?

There were billions of books in the world.

We might have to evaluate every single one, one at a time, to determine if they contained anything we could use.

My heart contracted. I sat at the table, my eyes looking at the spines.

The more I thought about it, the more the odds seemed completely impossible.

If magic really had been lost, how were we ever supposed to resurrect it? How could we ever find what we needed to bring it back?

"Is there something in particular I can help you find?" the librarian asked, coming to stand beside me. She looked down at me with concerned eyes.

"No, thank you," I said, wishing she could. But how would I ever ask?

She simply gave a nod and went back to her little table against the wall.

I stood and walked out of the room. In the hallway, I turned, looking in every direction.

I didn't know where to start. Here, in this library alone, there were somewhere around seventeen million books. This was the third largest library in the entire

United States, only trailing the Library of Congress and the New York Public Library.

There were thousands of rare manuscripts here. Surely there had to be something of value within these walls.

But I could spend my entire life here searching. And I didn't even live here in Boston.

Suddenly our library at Alderidge University seemed miniscule.

I raised my chin and took a deep breath.

We could only start with the resources at hand. Already, Nathaniel had discovered the book of telekinesis. We would tackle Alderidge's books, and then we would branch out.

Even though it felt like there would never be enough time, I reminded myself that we were still young. I was only just now nineteen, Nathaniel not even quite twenty-two. We had our entire lives, if necessary.

I blushed at the thought, at how easily I'd lumped us together for the rest of our lives.

I turned on my heel and headed off down the hall, to search for my father.

I THOUGHT I was a fairly good actress. Despite being overwhelmed and disappointed at my realization earlier, I thought I put on a good face and pulled myself back to my earlier excited mood. Once I'd found Dad, we headed out of the library and aimed for our favorite place to get clam chowder and Boston cream pie.

We'd eaten and all the employees came to sing to me when Dad told them what day it was. And then we'd walked slowly back toward the car, enjoying the lights of the city at night.

It had been a pretty great day, a great birthday, and a good way to embark upon my new life.

My tiredness hit me on our drive back down to Harrington. I sat in my seat with my head against the cool glass window. My father listened to the radio. I wondered if he went to bed mentally exhausted every single night. He was always filling his mind with endless information, history, facts, current events, fiction. I didn't know how he could fit it all in his head.

I hoped I could be like him someday. That I never, ever stopped being thirsty for knowledge.

We pulled up to the house just a few minutes before midnight. We parked in the driveway and my father wrapped his arms around my shoulders as we walked up to the door.

"Was it an okay birthday?" my dad asked, keeping his voice quiet so we didn't wake up the neighboring professors.

"It was great," I said, smiling up at him. "Thank you for a wonderful day."

He smiled and pressed a kiss to my forehead. "Nineteen. You're making me an old man, Margot."

I laughed, happy and sleepy.

Dad reached forward with the keys to unlock the door when he stopped. I leaned to the side to see what he was looking at.

There was something on the front steps. As I got closer, I saw that it was a stack of four books. They'd been tied together with a piece of twine, in a neat bow on top. And there was a single pink flower, the stem slipped under the twine.

There was a folded piece of paper under the bow.

"I believe this is for you," my father said as he picked it up and handed it to me with a little smile.

To Margot, from Nathaniel. Happy Birthday.

The words were written in neat, loopy handwriting that fit him in a way that was almost cliché.

A little smile pulled on my lips.

My father just smirked as he unlocked the door and turned the knob to let us in.

We stepped inside and it was all I could do to not run up the stairs and tear into the note.

"Thank you, again, for a wonderful day. And for the journal," I said, wrapping an arm around my father's waist. "I really do love it."

"You're welcome," he said, kissing me on top of the head. "Night, Margot."

"Goodnight," I said, smiling appreciatively as I walked to the stairs.

I closed my bedroom door when I stepped inside and turned on the lamp next to my bed. I sat down on the bed, holding Nathaniel's carefully prepared package on my lap. I hated to disturb it, but I untied the twine and it fell to a pile around the books. Smiling, I took the flower and laid it on my nightstand.

The paper crinkled as I unfolded it, and I remembered how I'd watched him fold the crane. This one had been folded into a star.

Happy Birthday, Margot. I hope you had a wonderful day with your father. While I don't have much money to spare, I wanted to get you something. Each of these books is a favorite of mine, from my personal collection. I think you will understand what a sacrifice this is. I hope you will read them and share your thoughts. I quite enjoyed "losing time talking about books."

I smiled and a little laugh bubbled up from my lungs. I brought my fingers to my lips, brushing over them.

Yours truly,
Nathaniel

Carefully, I folded the piece of paper back into its

star shape. I pulled the drawer of my nightstand open and carefully set the note inside.

I looked at each of the titles. They were all old, all books I'd never even heard of. Two of them sounded dangerously like love stories.

But I did understand the sacrifice Nathaniel had made in giving them to me. I understood that he'd given me a little piece of himself by giving me his favorite books.

I laid back in the bed and opened the cover of the first one and started reading.

CHAPTER EIGHT

Latin was very long the next day. I knew everything, so the material wasn't enough to hold my attention. I tapped my pen on my notebook over and over, wishing time would go faster. My writing class was marginally better. We got a big assignment and the last thirty minutes was devoted to starting the project.

I had no idea if what I wrote was any good, but there were words on the page at the end of the class.

I darted from my class out into the hall, looking up and down, hoping to catch a glimpse of Nathaniel. But he was nowhere to be seen.

I'd never resented a class so much as I did Social Studies. I felt myself glaring at the professor the entire time, wishing he would talk faster. It wasn't his fault I was anxious, but it was his fault for giving such a boring lecture that I had no interest in listening to a single word he said.

The moment the class was over I yanked my bag over my shoulder and headed out into the hall.

I realized then I should have taken the time to ask about Nathaniel's class schedule. I didn't know any of his classes. I didn't know what professors he had, so I couldn't even take any guesses.

But most of the history classes were on the far end of the building, so I started making my way there.

I was halfway there, cutting through the common room, when I spotted Nathaniel across the space.

I couldn't help it when a girlish smile pulled on my lips and I quickened my pace.

"Hey," I said, putting my hand on his shoulder.

But my smile immediately died when he turned around and I got a good look at his face.

There was a bruise forming around his right eye and his upper lip was split.

Nathaniel's eyes darted away from me, looking out over the crowd.

"Oh my gosh," I breathed. On instinct, both my hands came to either side of his face and I guided his gaze back to me as I looked at the black eye. "What happened?"

"Nothing," he replied automatically as his eyes wandered away from me again. "Just a run in with the Society Boys. It wasn't a big deal."

"No big deal?" I said, my tone rising, drawing a few looks from those around us. "Look at you! Why did they do this?"

Nathaniel's eyes flicked to meet mine again for just a brief moment. But it was just long enough that I understood everything.

They'd gone after Nathaniel because of what I'd said on the beach.

"Which one was it?" I asked. I didn't let go of Nathaniel's face. The distance between our bodies grew smaller and smaller. "David? James? Borden?"

Nathaniel reached up and wrapped his hands around my wrists, which instantly sent a wave of goosebumps over my skin. "It was nothing, Margot. Please, just leave it alone."

My jaw clenched and loosened, and I could see it in his eyes when he realized his request was never going to happen.

I turned away from him, but he kept one hand wrapped around my wrist. My eyes scanned the crowd as they all walked to and from classes, going every direction.

And there, across the way, I spotted them. David Sinclair and Borden Stewart.

"You two," I said loudly. Nathaniel's grip on my wrist tightened, a plea to not do this. But I yanked out of his grasp and stepped forward. I could swear I could see red as I stormed between the crowd that had paused to stare.

David and Borden both stopped, their eyes looking for me in the crowd. It didn't take long for them to find me.

A smug smile took shape on David's face. Borden's lips thinned out and he swallowed once.

I walked right up to the two of them. I got within two feet of their faces.

"Are your egos really that tender?" I asked, my heated gaze sliding from Borden to David. "That a few words of opposition spoken on a sunny day at the beach made you retaliate against one man, alone? How many of your Boys did you take with you, huh? Did you feel like the big man when you all went up against him by himself? Do you feel better now?"

David opened his mouth to speak, but I took another step closer, getting right up in his face.

"If you have a problem with me and my mouth, you can come to me and deal with your insecurity," I said, my voice dropping lower, because I knew that the entire room was listening. "But if you ever touch him again because of something you didn't like coming from my mouth, I'll go to Dean Lowell and tell him about that time you slid a hand up my skirt in the library, and you'll be gone before morning, shame on the name Sinclair forever."

"I never—" David began to say, but I cut him off.

"But Dean Lowell is a very old family friend," I said, letting a wicked smile begin to curl on my lips. "He's known me since I was born. And who do you think he's going to believe? Someone who's practically family, or the rich boy who has to buy good grades to keep his family proud?"

David glared at me, but I saw the fear in his eyes.

Something in me liked that I could make someone like him feel that way.

"Don't ever touch Nathaniel again," I said, glaring at him with venom. My eyes slid to Borden, who stood there silent with an unreadable expression. I glared at him, looking him up and down, trying to get a read on him. When I couldn't, I looked back to David.

He was scared. But I also saw a promise in his eyes, that somehow he would try and find a way to make me pay.

I made a deal with myself then. I'd be ready when he came after me.

But I meant it. If he went after Nathaniel again, I'd get him kicked out of Alderidge for good.

I turned and walked away from the leaders of the

Society Boys. The entire room was dead silent now, every pair of eyes on me. I let my hips sway just a little. I held my chin high.

I wasn't this kind of person.

I was a good girl who was a good daughter and a good student.

I'd never even been tardy to a class.

But something protective and fierce had woken in me since that day on the beach.

Nathaniel fixed his eyes on me as I walked to him. I couldn't quite read his expression.

But I didn't hesitate as I reached for his hand. I made sure everyone could see. I leaned into him just a little, and I flaunted my boldness in their faces.

I pulled Nathaniel after me, in the direction of the library.

"So, let me get this straight," he said as soon as we were out of ear shot of the crowd erupting with gossip and opinions behind us. "I'm not allowed to try to protect you from the Society Boys, but you can publicly stand up to them, in front of a large portion of the school, defending me?"

A little smirk formed on my lips and two emotions warred in me. Amusement, but also a little bit of regret for my words before. I'd meant them. But maybe I'd been a little too sharp.

"David can't do anything to me," I said as I laced my fingers through Nathaniel's and continued at a quick clip toward the library. "I have too many connections here. And it was kind of fun, stepping up to battle."

"You're certainly no damsel in distress, Margot." I looked back to see a smile pulling on Nathaniel's lips. "More like a damsel with a dagger."

I smiled too, my heart fluttering in my chest.

We walked through the main doors of the library, and while I might not have known his class schedule yet, I did know he worked today. But we had a little bit of time. So, I cut down an aisle of books and set off down a hallway, toward the very back, the most remote corner of the library.

The Eidem Room was one of the least occupied rooms. It was more of an overflow room. The room where they put the difficult-to-define books, the books no one wanted to read, the ones that had been forgotten about.

But it was a bit larger than the others. There were two couches in the center of the room, pointed at each other, a coffee table in between them. A fireplace was against the far wall and this was one of the two that were still used. But not today. The weather was still nice.

The shelves wrapped around the outside walls. They weren't full. Not like the other rooms. They were only maybe a third filled.

I kind of felt bad for the Eidem family. All the rooms were named after families who had donated money or significant contributions to the school. It should have been prestigious. But this room was practically forgotten about.

As we stepped into the room, I closed the double glass doors behind us. I knew no one would be coming to interrupt us, but still, I liked the feeling of privacy it provided.

"I hope you had a good birthday yesterday," Nathaniel said. He walked into the room and automatically he started making his way around the room. He grabbed random books and opened them, studying them for a moment, before putting them back on the shelf and moving on to another.

"I did," I said with a smile. I knew I should be helping in the search, but instead I went to the couch and sat down, stretching my legs out along it. "Dad and I have gone up to Boston for my birthday the last few years."

"You like the city?" Nathaniel asked. He didn't look back at me, though. He kept looking through books, searching desperately for something beyond words.

"I love Boston," I said. With his back turned to me, I got the opportunity to observe him without him knowing. His shoulders were broad enough to impress. His arms were lean and strong. His waist was narrow. His legs were long and looked capable. He had a nice figure, and I wasn't embarrassed to be looking at him. "You don't?"

"It's not that," he said as he set another book back on the shelf. He reached for another. "I just prefer the slower lifestyle. Everyone is in a rush in the city."

He was right. Everyone was in a rush. Which was exciting and I kind of liked it. But it had been a relief when we got home last night, and I could take a deep breath without bumping into someone.

"Thank you for the gift," I said. My words got lower then, quieter. "I wasn't planning on it, but I was awake all night reading *Death of the Crows*."

Nathaniel looked over his shoulder then, a smirk pulling on his lips. He put the book in his hands back on the shelf and crossed over to the middle of the room. He took a seat on the opposite couch. He rested one arm along the back of it and crossed one ankle over the opposite knee.

He looked absolutely at home here. Like the gate keeper to all the world's knowledge.

"You liked it, then?" he asked.

I couldn't help it. A silly smile broke out on my

face. I looked away, shaking my head. "I absolutely loved it," I confessed. "It twisted my heart and shattered it and put it back together, but not in the same shape."

I fell in love with it a little bit right then. The smile on Nathaniel's face. It was hesitant but genuine. It touched his eyes, bringing out the light in them.

I took a mental picture and I stored it away in my heart.

"And what about the ending?" he asked. "Who was right? The witch or the widow?"

I knew he would ask, and I knew it was going to trigger a strong response in me. I launched into my opinion. He responded with his own. And back and forth we argued and discussed. And it was incredible and beautiful.

Then Nathaniel looked at his watch and swore, bolting to his feet.

He was late for his shift at the library.

"I'll walk with you," I said, stepping to his side. "I have a paper I need to work on. Maybe you could walk me home after your shift?"

Nathaniel met my eyes and a little smile started growing on his face.

"I'd be honored," he responded simply.

And side by side, we made our way back into the main area, our shoulders brushing as we walked.

I felt my face blush as he stepped up to the desk and I let my eyes linger a little too long as I turned and took my place at one of the study tables. I picked a spot where I could face the desk, yet a few rows back far enough to not be creepy. I set my bag down and pulled out my assignment.

I did work. The words formed in my brain and they traveled down through my arm to my hand and out my pencil onto the paper. I was smart. School had never been a struggle for me. I'd always gotten good grades, and even if my parents hadn't been professors, I most likely could have gotten a scholarship here to Alderidge.

So, I got my work done.

But I was distracted.

I kept looking up at Nathaniel. I found myself pausing, my pencil hovering over the paper, as I watched him work. He helped students find their books. He organized returns onto the cart. He made repairs to volumes that had been haphazardly tossed into bags.

I knew I was falling for him. I considered myself a somewhat self-aware person. So, I asked myself, why?

Was it simply because we both had these supernatural abilities?

I didn't think it had anything to do with that, actually.

I thought it had everything to do with his old ways, which matched my own. The way he spoke. His careful appearance. I thought it had to do with his quiet strength and independence. His calm nature in the face of horrible people. I thought it might have been his respect to my father and the way he had opened up to me the more I had gotten to know him.

Nathaniel had everything that had been missing for me in every other boy.

He was a rare find.

I tipped my head back down, smiling to my homework.

My pencil started scratching at the paper again.

A minute later, I startled when something slid across my page and landed right under my nose.

It was a paper airplane, folded to perfection.

My eyes darted up and across the large space, my eyes met Nathaniel's.

A small, knowing smile pulled in one corner of his mouth.

One mirrored on my own face.

I unfolded the paper and found his neat handwriting on the page.

How will you ever get any homework done when you're staring at the back of my head all evening? I'm messing up every bit of alphabetizing. You're very distracting, Margot Bell.

I knew my face broke out into a smile, so I kept my face down toward the paper.

I grabbed my pencil and quickly scrawled a response. *I am not staring. Get back to work and stop flattering yourself.*

The moment my pencil left the paper, it instantly folded itself back into a paper airplane and took off.

My eyes grew wide with shock and worry as I watched it dip low, trailing along the floor, headed back to the help desk. I looked around, making sure no one saw, and found that everyone's heads were turned down to their books or homework.

I looked back just in time to see the airplane rise up the side of the desk and skid along the surface to stop right in front of Nathaniel. He grabbed it and unfolded the airplane.

I immediately locked my eyes back on my homework and tried to concentrate.

I'd written one sentence when the airplane landed on my paper again. I unfolded it to see he'd written his response beneath mine.

Liar.

I chuckled, only to immediately be shushed by Mrs. Walker, who was down one of the aisles directly to the side of me.

I muttered an apology and grabbed the airplane, tucking it into my backpack.

I glanced up just once more. My eyes caught Nathaniel, already looking right at me. Really, I didn't need to blush any deeper, but I did. A small smile crossed his lips and his gaze lingered for just a moment longer. And then he got back to his work.

I pushed my papers, books, and backpack across the table. And then I stood up and walked around, sitting in the chair opposite of where I'd been sitting.

There, now neither of us would be as distracted.

I shook my head, and I got back to work.

THE SOFT BRUSH of something against my face fluttered my eyes open.

My neck hurt. A piece of paper stuck to my face for a moment before it fell back down to the table as I sat up.

Nathaniel's eyes leveled with mine. Sleepily, I blinked at him.

"Let's get you home and into a bed, Margot," he said softly.

Confused, I blinked, looking around.

I was still sitting at a table in the library. But where I could swear just a few moments ago there had been a dozen other students at the tables as well, they were now all empty. Normally, all of the green table lamps were turned on, and now there was only this one on the table just down from me.

It was quiet, quieter than the library normally was.

Looking around, I realized there was no one else here.

"What time is it?" I asked, realizing I'd fallen asleep working on my homework.

Maybe I shouldn't have stayed up the entire night before reading the book. But I didn't regret it.

"Ten o'clock," Nathaniel said. He gently gathered up my things and as my brain woke up, I helped him. We slid my books and papers into my bag, and I stood, pushing the chair back under the table. "Come on. I'll walk you home."

"Thanks," I offered, my brain still foggy with sleep.

Nathaniel flipped the last lamp off and we walked through the library in darkness. We pushed the doors open and stepped out into the hall. Here too, it was empty and abandoned.

"Do you have keys to the school?" I asked, surprised.

"Only for tonight," he answered. "When Mrs. Walker saw you were asleep at the table, I told her I'd walk you home and she gave me her keys to lock up. I'm supposed to return them first thing tomorrow."

"She must really trust you," I said as we headed

down the hall, to the front doors. "I doubt she's ever loaned out her school keys to anyone."

"I do my job well," he said, pushing the door open for me. I stepped through, out into the dark night. Nathaniel turned and the keys jingled as he fished for the right one. I heard the lock click into place and we turned out across the lawn again toward my house.

"My dad's going to want to put me on house arrest soon," I said, finding my house across the way, all of the lights still on. "I keep not being where I'm supposed to be."

"I think your dad trusts us," Nathaniel said, and through the dark, his shoulder brushed against mine.

I looked over at him. He didn't look back down at me, but I saw hints of a smile pulling on his lips.

"Us, huh?" I questioned.

The smile grew a little bit bigger. Through the dark, his hand found mine, and he laced our fingers together.

The contact between us sent every nerve in my body flying with the force of a flock of birds taking to the sky. My heart rate picked up. Even my scalp felt electric.

Despite all those reactions, I felt…good. I felt…peaceful.

I hugged my body a little tighter into Nathaniel's, and I felt him lean into me.

We turned the corner around the fence and set out

along the sidewalk. Suddenly, I wished I didn't live so close to the school, that this walk could last a few hours longer.

"I'm sorry if I made it harder for you to work today," I said as we slowed. My house was the next one. "I really didn't mean to distract you."

We came to a stop in front of my steps. "I'm not sorry," Nathaniel said. He looked down at me and something in me loved our difference in height. I loved the intense look in his eyes. I loved it when his other hand reached out for mine and he laced his fingers through that hand as well. "I kind of want you to study there every day I'm working in the library. But I would never want your inability to look away to interfere with your studies."

I huffed a laugh, letting my eyes fall down to the space between us in embarrassment.

But Nathaniel hooked his finger under my chin, tilting it back up to him.

"I really want to kiss you right now, Margot," he confessed, his words little more than a whisper, only real in this small space between us.

"I really wish you would just do it," I said, my heart racing painfully in my chest.

Nathaniel leaned forward, just slightly, and my eyes began to close. I was ready for the moment I'd secretly been daydreaming about for days now.

"I swear I will," he whispered instead. "But not when your father is sitting in the window."

Instantly, I whipped around, my eyes jumping to the front window.

Sure enough, there was the silhouette of my father, sitting in his chair. His back was to us in the window, but from how incredibly still he was, I had the feeling that he was straining to hear our every word.

A curse slipped out over my lips.

Why couldn't he just go to bed?

I looked back at Nathaniel. He wore a very annoying smile, as if he thought this was funny. I glared up at him. But he ran his hands up my arms and pulled me into his chest, wrapping me in an insanely arousing embrace.

"There's always tomorrow," Nathaniel said. He tucked his head low, pressing his cheek into the side of my head, so he spoke right next to my ear. "Or the next day, or the day after that."

"It better not take that long," I said, mock threats in my voice. "Or I might just lose interest and move on."

He chuckled, knowing I was just teasing. He released me, looking down into my eyes.

"Goodnight, Margot," he said, and everything in me loved and relished the way he spoke, his every syllable.

"Goodnight, Nathaniel," I said. And my heart broke a little bit when he stepped away. He walked back down the sidewalk backwards for five steps, holding my eyes the entire time. I stepped up onto the first step, and finally, he turned, and walked back to the school grounds.

I glared at my front door for a moment and let out an annoyed huff. I pulled the door open and stepped inside.

My father looked up at me with an expression of fake surprise. We stared at each other for a total of seven seconds, a battle of wills.

In the end, I just huffed another breath of annoyance and crossed the living room to the stairs and went up to bed.

Dad didn't say a word. But I heard him let out a chuckle once I reached the top of the stairs.

Emotions pulled me in every direction. I was elated from the path things were moving down, the way Nathaniel had taken my hand, his promise, but so annoyed the night hadn't ended the way I'd hoped.

I brushed my teeth with ferocity. I nearly ripped my pajamas in my violent effort to pull them on.

I almost knocked my lamp over as I roughly clicked it off.

I lay in bed, staring at the ceiling, replaying every

moment of the day, when there was a light tapping sound against my window.

My heart was instantly in my throat and I threw off the covers as I leapt from the bed.

A ridiculous smile crossed my face when through the window, I saw a paper airplane hovering outside. I threw the window open and it floated inside to land on the floor. Wildly, I searched around for Nathaniel, but I didn't see him anywhere in the dark.

With a smile, I sat on the floor and unfolded the airplane.

I swear, was all it read.

My entire chest was alight with excitement and joy. I scrambled across the floor to my desk and grabbed a pencil. Laying the paper flat on my wooden floor, I responded with just one word.

Good.

I carefully folded it back into its shape and went back to the window. Gently, I launched it out into the night air.

It glided through the air, dipping down and out. And then like a magical wind, it caught and changed direction, heading immediately in the direction of Nathaniel's solarium. It rose up and over the fence, and sailed over the lawn, directly toward the abandoned north wing of the University.

With a smile, I slid the window closed.

With my heart pounding and my mind whirling with anticipation, I crawled back into bed and pulled the covers up to my chest.

I lay there, smiling up at the ceiling, seeing nothing but Nathaniel's lips and intense eyes.

Guess I wouldn't be getting any sleep that night either.

CHAPTER NINE

I FELT STUPID THE NEXT DAY.

I'd searched for Nathaniel in the halls before and after each of my classes. My heart had been hammering the entire time, my brain fixed on one thing and one thing only.

We were planning to kiss. Soon.

How juvenile was that?

Who plans out their first kiss?

It was something that should happen in the heat of the moment. Not something that was scheduled out on the calendar with a date and a time.

I'd shaken my head at myself after my last class. I really debated just going home right then and putting myself in seclusion until I could get my head on straight.

But still, I found my feet pointed in the direction of the library.

I was halfway there when I heard a set of determined footsteps walking up behind me. And my skin went cold when I looked over to find David Sinclair walking right beside me.

"You've got spunk, Margot," he said, walking quick to keep up with me. "You're not afraid to speak your mind and you can take charge even with everyone watching and waiting for you to screw up."

"What do you want, David?" I asked, my tone even and cold.

He grabbed my arm then, pulling me to a stop and stepping to the side of the hall to let the other students by.

"I want you by my side," he said. He fixed me with his blue eyes, and in them, I saw that he was absolutely serious. "You and I…" He shook his head. "I'm going to be a powerful man someday, Margot. Just like my father. And while I might love my mother, she only ever wished to be at home making baby after baby and cooking award winning pies. But you and I, as a team? We could be the type that makes history."

I pressed my lips together, letting out a hard breath through my nose. I stared into those blue eyes, looking over his face, his expression. David wasn't particularly tall, though he still had a few inches on me. But he kept himself very physically fit to make up for it. He was always out running or at the gym, or at the school's pool.

He wore the nicest suits in school. His hair was always perfectly slicked back, the products gleaming against his dark hair.

He looked like a powerful man already.

"Some girls might throw themselves at you because, you're right, we all know you're going to be a powerful, rich man someday," I said, my eyes rising back up to meet his. "But there are more important qualities. You've been an asshole your whole life, David Sinclair. You're cruel and you're vain and you think people will bow down to you. The wild thing is that you're capable of changing all of that in a heartbeat. You could wake up tomorrow and decide you want to be a better person. But I don't see that happening."

I took a step back from him, out of his reach. His eyes widened slightly, and I watched as his jaw grew hard and tight.

"I would say I'm flattered by your offer, but I'm really not," I said, shaking my head just once.

From across the hall, I saw his henchmen, James and Borden. They watched our exchange, and I would guess they had heard every single word.

But it didn't change my response.

"Think about what kind of man you really want to

be, David," I said, turning down the hall again. "You don't have to be the person you are today."

I turned my back on the leader of the Society Boys, a man who would indeed be powerful and rich someday.

Maybe he'd come after me.

Maybe he'd try to punish me for the words I'd just spoken.

But I'd learned something about myself in the past few weeks.

That I would never bow down to bullies. I enjoyed a good verbal spar. And I wasn't afraid of his retaliation.

The halls were exceptionally crowded as I made my way toward the library. Students rushed between classes or headed to the cafeteria for lunch. We were all focused, driven, motivated to see our futures develop into something great due to our time spent in these halls.

I pushed my way through the last of the crowd and got to the doors of the library. They swung open without even a creak.

It was quiet in here. The lighting was dim. The only natural light came in through the stained-glass windows above the circulation desk, and it was overcast that day. The green lamps on the study desks cast the space in eerie light. I stepped inside and made my way between rows of tables. I went up to the desk, where Mrs. Walker was busy organizing the title cards.

"Afternoon, Margot," she greeted me with only a quick glance up. "You've always been a reader, but it seems you've been spending a little more time than normal within our hallowed walls."

"Is Nathaniel working?" I asked, ignoring her awkward tease.

"His shift starts in an hour," she responded simply. She turned and went to work on the new arrivals waiting for her on the counter.

I aimed for the aisles, wandering while I waited for Nathaniel to arrive. I walked past the mystery section, past the thrillers. I stepped into the science fiction aisles. Then into the fantasy. I didn't know what I was looking for. Nothing really. I still had three more books at home, the ones Nathaniel had given me. They were a high priority, because if the others were as good as the first one I'd read, I was anxious to dive in.

But these were books, and they'd been my best friends since I learned how to read. My fingers trailed along the spines, my eyes reading titles.

I'd always been drawn to old books. I loved the way their spines were worn. How there were no pictures on them, so it was only about the content. I loved the gold foil pressed into the titles. I loved the way the pages yellowed and how they smelled. I loved finding little notes in the beginning, gifting notes or dedications.

I pulled one off the shelf, one whose title was almost impossible to read. I skimmed through it and set it back on the shelf. I plucked another out and started reading the first few paragraphs. A few minutes later, I set it back when it failed to pull me in.

I wandered farther down the aisle, my eyes skimming up and down, searching for interesting spines.

One on the second to bottom shelf pulled my attention. The spine was an old yellow and it bore no title at all. It was thin, the pages short. I bent down and pulled it off the shelf.

The Coin of Compulsion, the title read. But there was no copyright page. No author was noted. And it was all handwritten.

I turned the page and found it was all in poem format.

It told the story of a rich, lonely young man who could not find an honest wife. He'd courted many women but when they got close to their wedding, he found each of them had lied to him about something important. One had already been married and was trying to steal his money. One was simply up for the challenge of winning him over. And one was simply tired of working and wanted a man to take over.

So the young man had bewitched seven coins, so that when he gave the coin to someone, they could only tell him the truth.

With each new woman he courted, he gave them a coin and they all revealed their truths, ugly and sinister.

Finally, with the seventh, he found an old friend who confessed that she had loved him her entire life but was too scared to say anything. She wanted nothing from him but his love.

They married and lived happily ever after.

I couldn't decide how I felt about the young man's actions as I came to the end of the poem. No one wanted to be lied to, but forcing everyone to tell the truth, when they didn't know he was making them? I didn't know what was right or wrong.

I went to set the book back on the shelf when my fingers turned the page. There were always a few blank pages at the end of a book. But with this one, I found more writing on those last few pages.

To bewitch the coins, the bearer must grasp the coin in their hand and confess one truth to the coin. Upon giving the coin of compulsion to another, they will be unable to lie to you for the rest of the day.

My heart beat hard in my chest. Blood raged in my ears.

I looked up, though my eyes fixed on nothing but the books on the shelves.

These felt like instructions.

The handwritten story.

The unnamed author.

I stood up straight, looking down the aisle, back toward the study desks.

My boots clicked on the wooden floor as I nearly ran down the aisle. And just as I stepped out into the study hall, I ran straight into Nathaniel, on his way to the help desk.

"I think I found another," I blurted in a harsh whisper. I grabbed his hand, yanking him down the aisle. With bewildered eyes, he looked down at the yellow book in my hands. "It's written by hand and it tells this terrible story, but at the end…" I looked up at Nathaniel, knowing my expression must be wild and crazed. "There are instructions."

I knew I hadn't really explained everything, but my mind was racing too fast to make a logical presentation. I was searching my room mentally for any coins. Pennies, quarters, nickels. I knew there wouldn't be much, but I had to have some.

"You're sure?" Nathaniel asked. His voice was breathy. He indicated for the book and I handed it over without thought. "It's…it's not like the other one. No glamour."

"Why would they all be that way?" I challenged. "There could be hundreds of different authors, all of them teaching different things. Not every mage would have thought to hide their writing."

Nathaniel's eyes rose and they searched the aisle behind me, though I knew he wasn't really looking for anything. I saw wild excitement building in his own eyes. He seemed taller in that moment. His shoulders seemed to broaden.

"Do you have to be anywhere this afternoon?" he asked, his eyes dropping back to me.

"No," I said, a smile starting to grow on my face.

One mirrored on his. He handed the book back to me. "I'm going to tell Mrs. Walker I'm not feeling well. Meet me at my place in ten minutes?"

I nodded once, smiling like a lunatic. He turned, heading for the desk. I turned for the exit, carefully slipping the yellow book into my bag.

The clouds overhead were growing thicker and thicker. The wind started picking up, and I could tell a storm was on its way in. I picked up my pace and was running by the time I got to the fence that sectioned off the ruined north end of the University.

The first few drops started to fall as I cut into the overgrown, abandoned garden. And by the time I saw the solarium, fat rain started pouring from overhead. I yanked the door open and stepped inside, shaking the rain off me.

Glancing around, I saw that it looked exactly the

same as the other day. It was still cozy and comfortable. It still smelled exactly like him.

But it was darker today with the clouds overhead. It was kind of beautiful, seeing the rain hitting the sloped glass roof.

I'd just slipped my bag off and set it on the empty desk, when the door opened again, and a drenched Nathaniel stepped inside.

Rivers of rain ran down Nathaniel's face, and his suit jacket was entirely soaked. He peeled it off and carefully hung it on the coat stand beside the door and started unbuttoning his shirt.

There was a blush on Nathaniel's cheeks as his eyes met mine. He turned away, stepping up to the dresser beside his bed.

That didn't mean I looked away as he peeled his shirt off and rummaged around for a new shirt.

There were scars laced all over Nathaniel's back. I didn't know how they'd gotten there, but my imagination took off, coming up with stories of abusive foster parents and violent boys in group homes, of his biological drug addicted parents hurting him.

It took everything I had not to cross the space and wrap my arms around him right then.

Nathaniel pulled a simple long-sleeved gray shirt over his head and then ran his hands through his wet hair.

It was longer than I realized, and there was a wave to it on the ends. I kind of liked it a little wild and disheveled like this.

"Let's take a look at that book, shall we?" Nathaniel said.

I nodded and pulled it out of my bag. Together, we settled onto the couch. Nathaniel opened it to the title page.

The Coins of Compulsion, the title read again, fitting and perfect, now that I knew its story's content.

"Is there an author listed in the book about telekinesis?" I asked as my eyes drifted down to where there should have been an author credited.

"Yes," Nathaniel responded without much thought. He was flipping the page and moving on to the next. "Alexander Wolfram."

"That sounds German," I said, looking over at him.

"Wolfram certainly is," Nathaniel said. He was talking, but I saw his eyes reading. "But Alexander typically isn't. I'm still working on figuring out his ancestry."

I smiled. Nathaniel's dedication to family history and history in general was beautiful.

He flipped the page again and this time I read along, trying to memorize the words on the page.

When we got to the instruction pages, Nathaniel read them out loud. He stood as he did so and went to the shelves that lined the wall next to his bed, above his dresser and rack that held his suits. He grabbed a jar there and as he came back to the couch, I saw that it was filled with change.

When he finished reading the instructions, he looked up at me.

"What do you think?" I asked. My heart was racing. "Is it real?"

"Only one way to find out," he said, his words breathy with excitement.

He reached into the jar and drew out two coins. He placed one in my hand and wrapped his long fingers around his own.

"Wait," I said, interrupting him before he could speak to the coin. "The only way we can test this, right now, is on each other."

Nathaniel looked over at me, and I could tell from his expression that he hadn't even thought about that yet.

"I…I'm okay with it," I said. "I just want to make sure we're both prepared for the consequences of the next twenty-four hours of absolute honesty. This might turn into more than we asked for."

Nathaniel looked at me for a long moment. I watched as his eyes fell from mine, down to my lips. A hunger woke up in my lower belly and I found myself leaning forward just a bit.

"I still really want to kiss you right now, Margot," he said. He had leaned in slightly closer too, and our lips were only inches apart. "But maybe it's best we wait. What if things come to light because of this and one or both of us changes our minds about what we want?"

His words made my stomach feel sick. I felt them sinking down in me with a heavy coldness. I shook my head. "Don't say that."

I could nearly hear him saying the words, *but they might*, even though he didn't say them out loud. But he simply gave a nod.

We both looked down at the coins in our hands and a long moment passed while we both considered if it was worth it or not.

I closed my hands around the coin and brought my fist up to my lips.

"I always wanted to be a ballerina when I was a little girl," I said the first simple truth that came to my mind.

Nathaniel looked over at me, a surprised smile pulling at his lips. I shrugged in admission.

He held his own fist up to his lips and whispered to his coin. "I always wanted to be a samurai when I was a boy, so I could protect myself."

Nathaniel's confession broke my heart, especially considering the scars I'd just seen on his body.

I opened my fist and the penny lay on my hand, looking absolutely normal and ordinary. Nathaniel lay his open, and it looked just the same.

"Who wants to go first?" I asked, and even though I said I was okay with it, this did make me uncomfortable. People lie and keep secrets to protect themselves. I'd never thought of myself as a liar, but people twist things all the time to help themselves out.

What wasn't I being honest about, and hadn't even given a second thought to?

"I will," Nathaniel said. He lay his own supposedly enchanted coin on the coffee table, next to the jar of change. He set the book down next to them.

He held his hand out and locked his eyes with mine.

He wasn't afraid.

He wasn't hesitating.

But I did. I held the coin in my hand for three long seconds, hoping and praying that this wasn't a terrible, horrible idea.

Holding my breath, I laid the coin in the middle of Nathaniel's palm and pulled my hands back to my chest. They shook as I clutched them together.

"Ask me something and I will try to give an answer that is a lie," he said.

I wished I had his confidence.

I racked my brain, trying to come up with

something simple. Something that couldn't possibly ruin anything.

"Do you like broccoli?" I came up with, and instantly felt embarrassed about it.

"No," he said the words without hesitating.

I blinked at him for two seconds, racking my brain, trying to come up with a way to definitively test this.

"Is that the truth or is that the lie?" I asked.

Nathaniel blinked and looked down at the penny in his hand. "That's the truth. I really do hate broccoli. I tried to tell you I like it, but the words changed to the truth the second they hit my tongue."

His eyes flicked up to mine, and they filled with excitement. "Ask me something else. Something I could easily lie about."

I sat back on the couch, folding my legs up under me. I faced directly at him and he shifted toward me. Our knees touched.

"Is your name Nathaniel Nightingale?" I asked, knowing it should be the easiest thing in the world to answer no.

"Yes," he responded. And looking at his mouth as he formed the word, I could see that it came out strange. Like he really was trying to say something else.

"You are not a student at Alderidge University," I said, trying a different method.

"Yes, I am," he corrected. His brows crept up a fraction of an inch.

"You hate spending time at the library," I said, pushing it a little further.

"No, I do not," he said with a chuckle.

"Who gave you those scars?" I asked. And as soon as they left my mouth, I wished I could shove them back in and swallow them out of existence. They'd left my mouth without my permission, a true test to see if he could lie to me or not, or simply not answer the question. Because I knew, I knew, he wouldn't want to answer the question.

"My parents," he said. Instantly, Nathaniel's expression sobered. I saw distance creep into his eyes. He leaned back a little. One of his hands rose up to cover the place where I'd seen a scar on his lower stomach. "One of them threw something at me. I don't remember what. They should have taken me to get stitches, but they didn't."

His hand moved to another scar that laced across his back. "A boy from the group home, when I was fourteen. I was new. I thought no one had claimed a bed, so I took it. I was wrong. He had a knife."

A hand came to my mouth to cover it to hold in the cry that ripped through me. I shook my head. Tears pricked the backs of my eyes and welled. "I'm sorry," I said, shaking my head. "I...I don't want to do this anymore. I didn't mean..."

Nathaniel sat forward and pulled my hand away. His eyes were still dark, and he looked down in his lap. But I felt calm radiating off him. "It's okay, Margot. I've never had someone who cared enough to talk about these things. But I don't mind talking about them with you."

And I knew it, because I knew the sincerity in Nathaniel's voice, and I knew because I had compelled him to tell the truth, that he meant what he said.

I leaned forward and wrapped my arms around him, hugging him tightly to me. "I'm so sorry, Nathaniel," I said as he wrapped his arms around me too, "that you had to go through all of that. It's not fair. You were just a kid. You should have been able to feel safe and loved."

He didn't say anything, but he ran a hand down the back of my head, over my hair.

"I want everything to be different for you now," I confessed, even though I hadn't been compelled. "I want you to know that you are wanted and appreciated and admired. And I think you're incredible, for walking through all that fire and coming out the way you did."

We both sat back, and Nathaniel looked into both of my eyes. He held onto one of my hands and brought it up to his cheek, laying my palm flat against the side of his jaw.

"You're the most incredible creature I've ever met, Margot Bell," he said as his eyes slid closed for a moment. "I feel as if you've become a drug I've formed an addiction to. I want you around, all the time. Every morning and every afternoon. The nights are incredibly long." His eyes slid back open. I saw then there was something more he wanted to say, but he held them back.

And I wondered how it scientifically worked. If I asked him directly what he was just going to say, he would have to tell me? But because I hadn't directly asked, could he withhold the information?

I didn't push it further.

"I'm not sure how this works," I said. "If you have to give that coin to me, or if I pick it up, will it just work?"

So, I decided to test it. I picked it up off of the coffee table and held it in my hand.

"Ask me something," I said.

Nathaniel squared off with me. "Is your name Margot Bell?"

"No," I blurted instantly.

Nathaniel's eyebrows rose half an inch instantly. "Interesting," he said.

I handed the penny back to Nathaniel. "So, you have to directly give it to me, then?"

"I suppose," he said. Easy and simple, he handed me the coin. I wrapped my fingers around it.

"Is your name Margot Bell?" he asked me once more.

"Yes," I said. And as I said them, something on my tongue felt bitter and sharp. I was going to say no, but the word literally transformed on my tongue, coming out as the truth.

"Is your father Professor Arthur Bell?" he asked, a smile forming.

"Yes," I answered, even though it wasn't the word I was sending down to my lips.

"And you're absolutely bored with your school load this semester, because you could have passed all of these classes as a high school sophomore," he said as a statement.

"Yes," I said, sounding ridiculously arrogant. I brought my hands up and covered my mouth as my eyes grew wide.

Nathaniel laughed, shaking his head. With wonder, he grabbed the yellow book from the coffee table once more. "It works," he said, smiling a full smile. "It's going to be agony for me, not knowing who the author of this was."

"There has to be others here," I said, shifting

forward. "If we've found two books in the span of a few months, there has to be more. And dozens, maybe hundreds of others in this region. We aren't even in an area where there were witch trials. What might we find in Salem? Or the Boston Public Library?"

"It might take us our entire lives to find them, though," Nathaniel said, coming to the same realization I had. "At least with the glamour it was a quick way to tell. If they aren't all that way…" he shook his head. "We could spend our entire lifetime reading every single book in the world trying to divulge if the book contains magical instructions, and we'd only ever get through a tiny fraction."

I reached out and took Nathaniel's hand. "We've already found two books. And it's a good thing you and I both like to read."

He consented a smile, his eyes drifting back to his bookcases filled with all the books he'd read.

A thought rang in the back of my mind, and that bitter taste in my mouth that I just realized tasted like pennies, tried to immediately push the words out. "I…" I stuttered, trying to find the best way to say them. "Nathaniel, I'm thinking about telling my dad. About all of this. What you and I can do. The books."

His brows furrowed as he looked up at me.

"There's a chance he might be one of us," I said. "I know you think it came through my mother, and you're probably right. But there's a chance. And I feel like he deserves to know. Because after everything we've learned, which is nearly nothing, I have to think my mother's disappearance was because of magic."

The air grew heavy between us as it came to life. The thought had been there, in the back of my mind for a while. The circumstances leading up to my mother's disappearance had always been impossible. It made no sense. There had been no clues.

So, maybe magic had something to do with it.

"If she disappeared because of magic, he has a right to know. A right to some tiny shred of peace," I said. I started to feel desperate, hoping and praying Nathaniel would understand. I reached out and grabbed one of his hands, holding it in my lap. "And he might be able to help us. My father has read thousands of books in his life. What if he read a book, or books, and they were more than just that? He might know something without realizing it."

Nathaniel didn't react right away. He held my eyes and I could feel the thoughts turning over and over in his head. He considered all the options, all the outcomes.

"We need to be careful, Margot," he finally said. "I think we were hunted to extinction because of what we can do. Maybe they weren't careful enough before. I couldn't stand it if what we are puts you in danger."

His words sank down into my heart. "My father is the same way," I said. "He would never do anything to put me in danger. Or you. It's a little ridiculous how much he likes you."

He chucked once again, and I could tell from his eyes that he knew it was true.

"Alright," he said. "We'll bring your father into the loop and hope and pray he can help us."

I smiled, hugging Nathaniel in gratitude, even though I knew I didn't need his permission. If I wanted to tell my father, I would tell him. Only about me. But still. I was grateful to have Nathaniel's support.

"Now, what the hell do I tell him we are?" I said, resting my chin on Nathaniel's shoulder. "I don't even know what to call us."

Nathaniel leaned back and it was the most natural thing in the world when I curled up into his side and he slid his arm around my shoulders. I laid my head against his chest and he took my hand in his.

"History has always called them witches," Nathaniel said. "Whenever they hunted them, accused them, that's what they called them."

"I don't want to be burned as a witch at the stake," I confessed the words easily, still influenced by Nathaniel's coin of compulsion.

"So, the title of witch is out," he said without a fuss. "In fantasy they've been called warlocks. Wizards."

"Don't those both sound ridiculous to you?" I asked with a snort.

I felt it instead of saw it, Nathaniel's smile. "Maybe a little bit."

Nathaniel raised his free hand from around my shoulder, his fingers doing a little flick in the air. I heard a soft sliding sound, and just a second later, a book floated through the air and landed gently in his hand.

I laughed in delight, and the smile on Nathaniel's face made everything in my chest flutter.

It was a thesaurus. A fairly new edition I'd guess from the glossy cover and how straight all the pages still were. Nathaniel opened it toward the back and thumbed through pages until he got to a certain page in the W section.

Witch.

"Magician," he read off.

"Ta-da!" I said, pretending to pull a rabbit from a top hat. I shook my head.

"Conjurer or enchanter?" he asked.

I scrunched my nose and shook my head.

"Necromancer?" he read off in disgust. "I don't think either of us plans on raising the dead any time soon, if that's actually even possible."

"Pass," I said, nodding in creeped out agreement.

"Occultist," Nathaniel read off next.

"That sounds satanic," I said. "So far everything we've done feels more like scientific magic, not a deal with the devil in exchange for abilities."

"Occultist is out then," Nathaniel agreed. "Sorcerer?"

"Doesn't that sound a bit dramatic?" I asked, looking up at him and raising an eyebrow.

"You're being very picky about this," Nathaniel teased, but I could tell they were his honest thoughts.

"We're trying to resurrect magic here," I said as I sat up, mocking offense. "If I'm going to be this supernatural thing, I want to at least like the name the townsfolk are going to scream at me when they want me to hang."

From his expression, I didn't think Nathaniel liked what I said very much. But he didn't say anything. I relaxed back against his chest, my eyes going to the listed words beneath witch.

"What about mage?" I said when my eyes fixed on the word. They read it over and over again. I tried it out in my head. "It sounds more gender neutral. It's not overly dramatic. It doesn't sound like something the devil came up with."

"Mage," Nathaniel said. It was a word he'd said to me before. But we were trying to get more official with this. "It does sound better than all the other titles."

"I like it," I said. "You're a mage, Nathaniel Nightingale."

"And you're a mage, Margot Bell," he said, looking down at me. We both considered it for a moment. And then our eyes met.

"So, is that your official declaration for yourself?" Nathaniel asked.

I nodded. "I declare thee a mage, Nathaniel."

He chuckled and hugged me tighter for a moment.

Thunder cracked overhead just then. A little scream leapt from my lips, to my embarrassment. I'd been too in the moment. Enjoying Nathaniel's touch too much. Shaking my head, I stood, needing to put some space between Nathaniel and me.

He was right. Both of us wanted that kiss, but on a day like this, where anything could be said, where we could make each other be exceptionally honest, maybe it wasn't the right day.

"I think you should give me the telekinesis book," I said as I walked around the couch to face his bookshelves. "You've had it for months, and like you said, you practically have it memorized. I need to read the whole thing."

"Of course," Nathaniel said. He immediately stood and went to his bag that was hung on the coat tree by the door. He pulled the red book out of his bag and handed it over.

I ran my fingers over the cover and looked up at him.

Things felt different today. It felt like we were partners in this. We were equals.

"I'm really glad it's you," I confessed. "That you were the one who found this book, that you're the one who is like me. It could have been anyone. Most of us around here have roots back to the old settlers of the area. But I'm really glad it was you."

He stared at me, contemplating my words. I could tell he was fighting it again, the urge to kiss me. I wanted him to give in, but knew it was for the best that he didn't. "I'm exceptionally grateful it was you too, Margot."

This was going to be so annoying for the next twenty-three hours.

We needed a buffer.

"Let's go do it right now," I said. "Tell my dad. I think it will…help…in making it through this period of honesty and revelation. I want to do it together."

He blinked at me, and I saw him considering. I knew he was scared. This had been his secret, completely alone, for months. This was big. It had gotten hundreds, thousands of people killed in the past.

But I realized he trusted me.

"Okay," he said with a nod.

I looked at the time on the clock on the wall. It was nearly three o'clock.

"He'll be getting out of class in fifteen minutes," I said. "Let's go."

If I thought too much about it, I might talk myself out of it. I might second-guess myself. And I wanted to do this.

We left *The Coins of Compulsion* on Nathaniel's coffee table. I slipped the telekinesis book into my bag. Nathaniel pulled an umbrella off the coat rack, and together, we stepped back outside into the rain.

The garden was quickly turning into a muddy mess, but we stayed on the cobblestones that led to the opening in the fence. Out over the grass we set, and it wasn't long before my shoes were soaked, reaching all the way to my socks.

I hated wet feet almost more than anything.

There were dozens of students pouring out of the building by the time we reached the front doors. There were a few evening classes at Alderidge, but the majority of classes wrapped up by mid-afternoon. We fought our way through the bodies to step inside.

Nathaniel shook out the umbrella and closed it the second we stepped through the doors.

"Are you a superstitious person?" I asked as we set off down the hall toward my father's classroom.

"Logically, I shouldn't be," he said. "I know it's

ridiculous, but yes, I am a superstitious person."

"So, no walking under ladders?" I probed, knowing he would answer me completely honestly.

"Absolutely not," he said, shaking his head.

"No broken mirrors or black cats?" I teased.

"I would never get a cat anyway," he said, scrunching his nose. "I lived with a foster family once who had five cats. There was hair everywhere and the place smelled foul of urine."

"That's disgusting," I said. "What about dogs? Or are you just not a pet person?"

"I've always wanted a dog," he confessed. "A big one. I don't really care what breed. So long as it's as big as me when it stands on its hind legs."

I chuckled at his surprising answer. And I filed that information away for another time.

We turned down the hall and my eyes fixed on my father's classroom door.

Suddenly, I was nervous. Suddenly, I wasn't so sure about this.

I reached out and grabbed Nathaniel's hand, lacing my fingers through his. We stopped just to the side of his door and I turned into Nathaniel, my eyes falling to the floor.

Gently, I felt Nathaniel's index finger hook under my chin. He encouraged me to look up at him, but I didn't.

"You're right, Margot," he said instead. "If magic had anything to do with why your mother disappeared, your father has a right to know. Maybe him knowing will help him figure it out. If nothing else, it may help him get some closure."

Now I did finally look up at him. His green eyes were open and genuine and tender. I felt my soul latching onto his. He was like a song I couldn't get out of my head. One I played over and over until the words were no longer words anymore. They were just a part of who I was.

I reached up and placed my palm against the side of his jaw. I didn't say anything. I just studied his eyes, one and then the other. And then I leaned into him and wrapped my arms around him.

He rested his chin on the top of my head and wrapped his arms around me.

He felt good.

Warm. Peaceful.

He was kind of starting to feel like home.

The door to the classroom opened and students began to pour out. I regretted having to let Nathaniel go, but I stepped back, standing by his side. I kept one of his hands in mine.

Nearly two dozen students filed out of the classroom. My father's classes were popular. Arthur Bell was well liked in the school.

Finally, when they were all out of the way, I stepped into the doorway. I felt Nathaniel letting go of my hand, but I needed him. I grabbed hold of him tighter and pulled him in through the door after me.

Dad's classroom was one of the few circular auditoriums. There was a great big chalkboard at the front and three rows of seats circled around it, rising up with stairs.

He was inside, wiping writing off the chalkboard. I stood there with Nathaniel, staring at him, appreciating these last few moments before we changed his perception of his entire life.

Dad turned around and put a hand over his heart. "Margot, you startled me. Nathaniel, how are you?"

"Nervous," he said, giving an honest answer.

My father's brows furrowed, and he looked from Nathaniel to me, noting our hands were held together.

"Dad, we need to talk to you," I said, feeling my heart rate pick up. "There's something we need to tell you."

Instantly, his expression fell. Something grew dreadful and dark in his eyes. His shoulders even dropped.

"You're pregnant?" he said, and it bordered somewhere between a statement and a question. His expression grew angrier as his eyes slid from me to Nathaniel.

"What? No!" I startled, shaking my head.

"I swear, Arthur, we've never even kissed," Nathaniel said, raising up a hand as my father took one step forward. Apparently, there *were* limits to how much Dad liked Nathaniel.

My father stopped, his eyes flicking back and forth between the two of us. They dropped to our hands held between the two of us. "But you're together?"

Nathaniel and I looked at each other, and a surge of dread came up in me, because whatever was about to come out of our mouths, it was going to be exceptionally honest.

"We've certainly taken an interest in each other," Nathaniel said. "But we're trying to sort through some very heavy things first."

I kept my mouth closed somehow, but I looked back at my father and gave a nod.

"You two are being awfully dramatic about telling me you want to date," he said. He turned away from us and walked over to his desk next to the door that led to his actual office. "You're both level-headed adults. I think it's a good match, and I appreciate your concern for my approval, but if you want to be together, just do it."

I felt myself blushing, so I refused to look over at Nathaniel and get a read for how he was feeling. "Dad, that's not…" I shook my head. "That's not why we came to talk to you."

He stacked some papers on his desk before turning back to face us. There was still a look of doubt and questioning when he looked at us.

"It's about our ancestry," I said. My palms were sweating with nerves. Nathaniel squeezed my hand in support. "And the library. And maybe why mom disappeared."

That got his attention.

My dad sat up a little straighter. His eyes widened just a little bit. I saw his jaw clench tighter.

I finally let Nathaniel's hand go as I went to pull the telekinesis book from my bag. I held it delicately in my hands, looking at its worn, red cover.

He deserves to know, I mentally told myself.

I opened it to the middle of the book and took a step closer to him. "Can you read this book?" I asked.

His eyes fell to the pages. He took a moment to consider. "I recognize it as Gaelic, but I've never learned it. That…languages…that was your mothers' expertise."

I nodded, knowing everything he said already. I took another step toward him. "Touch the pages."

He looked at me with confusion at my strange request. But he trusted me. So, he reached up, and touched his fingers to the pages.

I watched his face the entire time. It didn't change. It only remained confused.

"Nothing changed," I said as a statement.

Still confused, my father's eyes rose back up to meet mine. He shook his head.

I pulled the book back to myself, turning it so that the words faced me. They were all in perfect English, entirely readable.

"Nathaniel found this book over the summer break," I began. "And yes, when it lays flat on a table, it's in Gaelic. But when either of us touches it, it's entirely in English. And it tells some incredible things."

I took a deep breath and looked back at Nathaniel. He gave me one nod, understanding.

He raised his right hand slightly. And then the paper on the top of the stack on my dad's desk folded. At the sound, my father looked down.

It began to fold itself into a complicated bird, different from the crane I'd seen him make.

My father took a step back from his desk. His eyes fixed on the bird magically folding before his eyes.

When it was finished, Nathaniel lifted his hands slightly, the air shimmering around it, and the bird took to the air. It flapped its wings and began to gently circle the classroom.

My father swore and staggered back from it, crashing into his desk.

"There's something in our blood," I said, my voice hoarse and scratchy. "I think it was in mom's, because it's in mine, too."

I focused on the dried flower in a vase on his desk, and I asked it to rise. It listened instantly. It rose into the air and it turned, end over end.

My hand was extended toward it, and gold swirled around my hand.

My father's eyes flicked from the rose to me. There was shock there, and maybe even a little fear. And from his expression, I knew. He'd had no idea before.

"I think that mom knew about this," I said. "And I think that somehow it was the reason she disappeared."

I LOOKED over at my father again as we walked across the wet grass. He stared down at the ground and he was so quiet. I barely even heard him breathing. His shoulders hardly moved as he walked. His hands were tucked into his front pockets. His brows were furrowed.

We'd told him everything. Everything we knew, all the things we could do, and I realized then how little that was.

We didn't know much of anything.

We didn't know our story.

We didn't know our limits.

But we'd told my father, and we'd told him that we thought it was the reason my mother had disappeared.

He'd said almost nothing. He'd sat or stood there, listening intently. He'd watched as we'd showed him what we could do. He listened as we told him about the books from the library. And when we asked him if he'd known anything else, he'd blinked a lot, and I could see him wracking his brain.

He said he'd go through Mom's family history more thoroughly. He said he'd have to look through his books and think about it, if there were any that were more than they seemed.

Nathaniel and I looked at each other and we knew we'd pushed him as far as we'd dared. So, as the sky outside the windows grew dark, I'd put a hand on Dad's back and told him we should go home and get him something to eat. He'd blankly nodded, and then we all walked for the doors.

I'd said goodnight to Nathaniel and watched as he walked across the lawn back toward the solarium.

Dad remained silent as we walked down the sidewalk and through the front door of the house. He sat in his usual chair in the living room, staring at his bookcases, while I set to making soup for dinner.

I started chiding myself as I cooked. I shouldn't have told him. This was too big. It broke his mind. I'd pushed him too far, because this involved my mother, who he loved more than anything in this world.

I should have just kept it to myself.

Why didn't I protect my father?

I was set to apologize to my father as I set his bowl down on the table. I determined to find some book that would teach me how to remove memories. I'd make him forget somehow. I'd make this right.

But when my father sat down at the table, he stared across the room and I could see he was in deep thought. His eyes were slightly narrowed. His hands were curled into loose fists.

I took a deep breath to apologize and somehow take it all back, when he suddenly launched into words.

"In the six months leading up to your mother's disappearance, she took trips up to Boston or Salem nearly every single weekend," he said. His eyes shifted over to me. "And she always came home with stacks of books. I didn't think anything about it at the time, because, well…" He gestured all around him, indicating the endless bookcases around our house, all filled with books. "But she never talked about them. She never shared them. What if…what if they weren't just any ordinary books?"

My heart thumped hard in my chest as I thought about it. Dad was right. We'd always taken a few trips a year up to Boston or somewhere else in the state, but in those last few months, she'd gone almost every weekend.

"Maybe she was searching the Boston Public Library," I said, realization dawning in my voice.

"Or going through old documents, records, books in Salem, where Mare McGregor had lived," Dad said. And as I looked at him, I saw hope dawning in his eyes. And excitement. "Your mother was the only person who rivaled me in reading. She could have found endless information about this…mage blood you must have shared."

Something tingled at the back of my brain. Something like hope.

"Do you know where she put all of those books?" I asked. My eyes cast around the house, wondering which ones she'd brought back with her from her search.

Dad shook his head. "Her classroom would have been my guess," he said. "But I cleared that out years ago. There was only what you'd expect. But the number of books your mother collected…" He looked around the house, too. "I know they aren't all here."

My heart started beating faster.

Because here it was, what our family had needed for so long. What Nathaniel and I desperately needed.

Hope.

We had hope for the first time.

CHAPTER TEN

We might have just shared earth-shattering news, but we all still had lives to live and responsibilities to take care of.

I went to class and did everything I was supposed to. Dad went to teach. I didn't see Nathaniel, but I knew where he would be. We all had lives to carry on with.

I kept my mouth shut and I avoided everyone I possibly could. We couldn't be exactly sure, but I was counting on the coin of compulsion's effects lasting twenty-four hours. I wasn't going to give David or Borden or anyone else the opportunity to bother me. I'd be brutally honest, more so than normal. And who knows what kind of situations would get me to confess one thing or another.

So, when school was over, I headed back home. Dad taught until five o'clock on Mondays, Wednesdays, and Fridays. So, I had the house to myself for a few hours.

Maybe I wasn't a good daughter, but maybe I was just doing what my father couldn't. I went straight for their bedroom. My mother's side of the room had been practically untouched since she disappeared. My father couldn't stand to disturb anything, maybe he thought she was going to come back any day and want her things just as she'd left them.

But I had to get some answers.

I had to know.

I went to her nightstand first. I went through the two books that sat atop it. One was written in French, and as far as I could tell, there was nothing more to it. The other was a book about the history of Massachusetts. It too, looked innocent.

I pulled her top drawer open. There was an assortment of pens and notebooks. Carefully, I went through each one. They were all notes from her classes, and her planner. I went through that carefully, but there was nothing that set off any alarms. Her appointments extended beyond the date she disappeared and tapered off in the months after.

That was another signal to me that she didn't plan to just walk away from her life.

The bottom drawer contained an assortment of memories. An old diploma. A clip of she and my father's wedding announcement in the paper. A few stacks of pictures, from before I was born, to ones just a year before she was gone.

I next moved to her dresser. Emotions pricked at the backs of my eyes as I carefully went through her clothes. They still smelled faintly of her. Like old books and lavender and jasmine. I remembered when she wore a certain blouse or the fuzzy socks she wore around the house. I remembered how pretty she looked in that dress.

But there was nothing more than memories and clothes in the dresser.

I snooped through her drawers in the bathroom next. All I found were old hair products and brushes, hair pins, her make up. There was a vial of her perfume sitting on a shelf, and for half a moment, I was tempted to spray some of it on, just to smell her again. But I wouldn't risk my father smelling it on me. I could only imagine what that would do to him.

I worked my way through the entire house, going from closets to the kitchen, to the sideboard in the dining room.

I found little pieces of her all around the house. Things that stirred memories. Things that made me smile. A lot of things that made me cry.

I walked to the living room and just stared at her chair by the window. My parents had bought a matching set a year before she disappeared and put them in the bay window. A small table sat in between them, and often, I'd find my parents holding hands over the table, reading quietly by candlelight.

I missed seeing them there together. I missed our normal. I missed when we didn't have this big gaping hole in our lives.

But I turned to the kitchen, because Dad would be home soon, and I knew he wasn't going to feel like cooking after getting home this late.

I had just finished making spaghetti when he walked in. He immediately launched into venting about a certain student. So, I sat there and listened while he ranted.

And for a minute, things did feel normal. They were the new normal.

Later, Dad retired to the living room. He had pulled out a stack of books from around the house that he wanted to take a closer look at as possibilities that could be more than they were.

I'd hesitated in the middle of the room for a solid thirty seconds.

My eyes were fixed on Mom's empty chair.

I'd only ever sat in it three times since she

disappeared. It just hadn't ever felt right. So, I'd sat on the couch every time I came in the living room.

But now, looking at it, I felt closer to her.

I felt the echo of her. As if she weren't that far away.

So, I crossed the room, and I sat down in it.

I worked on the pile with Dad. Book after book. I went through a dozen of them in twenty minutes.

But I was distracted. My mind was running a million different directions.

I shifted, crossing my legs, when something poked me in the hip.

I reached down and found a book had slid down into the crack of the cushion. I pulled it out.

It was some kind of fantasy novel. Thinking about it, I did recall Mom reading it soon before she disappeared. A bookmark poked out between the pages about two-thirds of the way through, telling me she never finished it.

"I've got some homework to work on," I said as I clutched it to my chest and stood. I pressed a kiss to my father's forehead. "See you in the morning."

"Night, Margot," he said, smiling as he watched me walk up the stairs.

I brushed my teeth and walked into my room with the book and my school bag. I set the book on the nightstand and dumped my school things out onto the bed.

I stood there for a solid thirty seconds with my hands on my hips. I let a huff of a breath out, feeling overwhelmed and bored at the same time.

With so much in front of us, it was nearly impossible to focus on school. And I felt it, a shift in the direction of my life. Things were bigger than I'd thought just a few weeks ago.

What did I want to do with my life now? Was it the same as what I'd wanted to do with it just a few weeks ago?

I told myself to suck it up and just focus on making it through the semester. I climbed onto the bed and got to work.

The sun had been down for maybe half an hour when I heard a light tap on my window.

I smiled before I even looked at it.

I slid the window open and a paper airplane floated right into my hands. Carefully, I opened it up.

I miss you, read Nathaniel's beautiful handwriting.

I smiled, instantly feeling better. Everything was heavy and complicated and overwhelming in my new world. But not Nathaniel.

Nathaniel felt good and exciting.

I haven't stopped thinking about you all day, or any other day, I wrote in return. As soon as the words were written on the paper, the airplane folded itself again and instantly shot back through the window.

I sat in my chair by the window, waiting and smiling to myself.

Two minutes ticked by, and then five. I started to get anxious.

Maybe the coin hadn't worn off. Maybe I'd been too honest. Maybe I was jumping too fast.

But then a noise outside drew my ear. I turned my head, listening closer.

And just two seconds later, Nathaniel's head emerged through my window.

"What are you doing?" I hissed, trying to keep my voice down as I sprang to my feet. I reached out a hand, helping him inside. He barely fit through.

His feet were louder than I would have liked as he stepped inside. He grabbed my shoulder to steady himself as he climbed through.

And in the dim light, our eyes met. His were so green and so intense. My stomach did a back roll.

"I couldn't wait one more hour," he breathed out. He took a step closer to me, and I watched as his eyes dropped down to my lips. "I'm pretty sure the coin has worn off, but that is the honest truth. I can't wait one more agonizing day, Margot."

I felt it building up inside of me. This surge of excitement. This was real. This wasn't a book. This was my story.

My hands came to the back of his neck, sliding up

into his hair. Nathaniel's hands came to my back, cradling me with a strength I didn't know he had. He stepped me back two steps, and just as he tipped us back onto the bed, his lips finally met mine.

This kiss was fierce. It was not elegant. It wasn't composed. Really, it was nothing like Nathaniel.

But I tasted him in every movement of his lips. I breathed him in. I touched him. His hands clung to me.

I let my lips slide open and I didn't know if he would take my invitation, but he did. His tongue sought out mine. Deeper and more desperate, the kiss evolved. His body pressed into mine, and despite our height difference, I felt that we fit together perfectly.

One of Nathaniel's hands ran up my side, slipping up along my arm. His fingers wrapped around my wrist and something in me thrilled at the motion.

My entire body was alight with need and want and utter satisfaction.

Finally. Finally.

I smiled under his lips. Gently, I rolled us so Nathaniel and I were both on our sides. Through the dim light, our kisses slowed and I rested a hand on his cheek as our eyes met once more.

"I want you, Margot," Nathaniel said. He rested his hand in the valley sloping down from my ribs and my hip. He touched the bare skin there from where my shirt had ridden up, and I'd never felt anything so good. "Every morning and every night and all the hours in between. I can't ever get you out of my head."

"Glad to hear I'm not the only one getting a bit obsessed," I said. I leaned forward, gently pressing my lips to his. My eyes slid closed in ecstasy and a smile pulled at my lips.

"Be mine, Margot," he said. He wrapped his hand around my wrist. He brought my palm to his lips, pressing a kiss there. And then he kissed each of my knuckles, one by one. "You've claimed me publicly on several occasions. Let me do the same, and let your words be the truth."

I held his eyes as I rolled him over onto his back. I climbed onto him, one knee on either side of his hips. I grabbed his wrists this time, pinning them above his head. And slowly, I lowered my mouth to his. I kissed his lips. And then I kissed the corner of his mouth. Then I kissed the side of his jaw. And finally, his neck.

"You belong to me, Nathaniel Nightingale," I said, whispering the words to the hollow below his ear. "And I'm yours."

He reached up as I released his wrists, lacing his fingers into my hair. He held my eyes with an intensity I'd yet seen from him. I saw hunger there. I saw claiming. I saw that he would fight, no matter the cost, for me.

So, I didn't hesitate as my mouth returned to his, hungrier and more confident than before. His lips weren't gentle. His grip was demanding. And I couldn't get enough of how his hands felt as they slid from my hair, down my shoulders, over my back, and to my hips.

Once more, Nathaniel rolled us, pinning me against the bed. His kisses trailed from my mouth, down to my neck. I relished in the feeling of his tongue on my skin and every inch of me set on fire.

I'd been kissed before. I'd kissed three other boys in high school. It had been nice, at times awkward and wet.

But nothing, *nothing* compared to kissing Nathaniel.

He had a hunger and I was filled with both the desire to fill it, and leave him starving, so that he would always come back for more. He was confident and exploratory. He knew what he wanted, and he knew I wanted it too and invited me on every inch of this journey.

His kisses trailed from my collarbone, across my chest, to the other side.

I threw out a hand to brace myself. Only I hit something on the nightstand.

It went flying through the air.

It hit the floor.

And then there was the sound of something metal hitting the wooden floor. It skittered across the floorboards and hit the opposite wall.

"You okay, Margot?"

My entire body tensed and grew cold at my father's voice just outside my bedroom door.

Nathaniel instantly grew still, holding his breath.

"Yeah," I said, and I knew my voice probably sounded desperate and sharp. "Just dropped my pen."

There was a slight pause, and I just about died, wondering if, somehow, he knew. If he knew I was lying flat on my back with Nathaniel Nightingale poised over me, one of his knees between my legs, his hand splayed over my ribs, his lips hovering over my neck.

He couldn't know.

He couldn't know.

But my heart was frozen in fear all the same.

"Alright," my father finally said. "I'm going to bed. Get some sleep."

"'K," I said, praying my voice didn't sound too strained.

We both listened hard to the sound of his footsteps walking away. Still, neither of us dared move as we listened to him in the bathroom. And we still didn't move until we heard his bedroom door close and sixty seconds passed by.

Nathaniel finally relaxed, laying the full weight of his body on top of me. He tilted his head down, resting his forehead against my shoulder with a sigh.

I couldn't help the smile on my face or the laugh that didn't leave my lips but shook my chest. Within five seconds, Nathaniel's did the exact same thing.

"Well, this turned into a much more interesting night than anticipated," I whispered.

Nathaniel just laughed again. He shook his head before he pressed a kiss to the side of my neck and then rolled off me. He lay on his back, crooking one arm above his head. The other fell over onto my middle and he found my hand, lacing his fingers through mine.

"Probably for the best he walked up here when he did," he said, his voice quiet and calm once more. "I was getting a little carried away."

I rolled over, angling toward him. "I certainly didn't mind."

He smiled on one side of his mouth. "I could tell. Still, I need you to know that I'm not this type of man. The kind who just crawls in through a woman's bedroom window and jumps into her bed. You seem to have brought out a new man in me, Margot."

I just smiled and leaned forward, kissing him once more, just because I could, and I really, really wanted to. "I kind of like who we are together. It feels real. Natural."

He didn't say anything, but the look in his eyes told me that he agreed.

Needing some air, I rolled away and turned on the lamp beside my bed. Sitting on the edge of it, my eyes searched the floor for whatever it was I'd knocked over.

Laying on the ground was the book I'd brought up, the one my mother had been reading. There was a card poking out of its pages. Picking it up, I found it was one of the title cards, for a book located in the McCallum room. But it certainly wasn't for the book she'd been reading. And I didn't know why she would have taken the card.

"You ever read either of these books?" I asked, my brows furrowed. I held the book and the card up.

Nathaniel took them and examined both. "I haven't. But this number…" he squinted his eyes, looking at the number on the card. "I swear it doesn't exist. And it doesn't even make sense with this asterisk."

My brows furrowed, trying to figure out what that meant.

But as I looked back at the floor, I saw something gleaming against the floorboard. I slid off the bed and crawled forward on my hands and knees. I grabbed it and sat back on my knees.

It was a key.

It was one of those older styles. Not the old skeleton keys, but the kind from the turn of the century with a loop on one end and a star shape on the other.

I looked back at Nathaniel, who looked down at the key with rapt interest.

My heart broke out into a race.

"My father said my mother had been collecting books from Boston and Salem before she disappeared," I blurted the words as they exploded in my head. "But he said they're not here, and they weren't in her office." I twisted around, kneeling at the side of the bed, holding the key up for Nathaniel to see closer. "What if…what if this opens some room? What if this is a clue?" I grabbed the card with the room location and the number Nathaniel didn't think existed.

Nathaniel looked back up at me. "Margot, what if she found things? What if she knew…everything?"

My eyes brightened. Hope and excitement surged in my veins. "Let's go," I said, getting to my feet. "We need to find it."

Nathaniel's hand snapped out, grabbing hold of my wrist. "The school has long been locked."

The truth of what he said hit me with a suffocating tidal wave. I sank back down onto the bed and my shoulders sagged with disappointment.

"So, it's a good thing I made a copy of Mrs. Walker's keys before I returned them to her."

My eyes flicked back over to Nathaniel, and my

excitement doubled at the coy mischief in his own. I felt a smile grow on my face and I twisted, crawling up into his lap. Anticipation and lust and excitement sparked in my lower belly, racing down my inner thighs before returning to my chest. I placed my hands on either side of his face, breathing him in as I kissed him.

I really, really loved us as a team.

"You ready?" I asked as I pulled away for breath and looked down into his eyes.

They danced with excitement and desire. But he nodded, a little smile forming on his lips.

I crawled off his lap and pulled him off of my bed, to his feet. I turned to the shelf to one side of my room and grabbed a flashlight, two candles, and a box of matches, just in case. I grabbed an empty shoulder bag from the hook on the wall and dumped them into it. Carefully, I set the novel, the card, and the key inside.

Nathaniel reached out for it and slung it over his shoulder and chest.

"Come on," I said, going to the window. Nathaniel stepped up to it and slipped out, lithe and elegant, like a leopard. He shimmied his way down the roofline a way and held out a hand for me.

It wasn't as easy as he made it look. I was terrified I would slip and fall right off the roof, but I made my way down to him, and watched as he stepped one foot back into the oak tree behind the house. He held out a hand and helped me do the same thing.

In two minutes, we were down on the ground. I slipped my hand in to his, and together, we set off at a jog down the sidewalk and hooked around the fence toward Alderidge. Hand in hand, we ran across the lawn, keeping an eye out for security guards.

My heart was racing by the time we made it to the doors. Nathaniel fished the key out from his pocket, and I kept watch while he fiddled with it. Relief washed over me when I heard the click. And I was eternally grateful that the grounds keepers kept the doors well-oiled when we pushed it open and it did not creak. We stepped inside and Nathaniel re-locked it behind us.

I'd been in Alderidge after hours plenty of times before. I'd even slept in my father's office overnight once. We'd stayed late and I'd helped him grade papers. We'd both fallen asleep and hadn't woken till morning.

But it felt different tonight. It felt like anything could happen. And suddenly the school felt much larger and foreign, having a key that opened some secret lock within it.

We cut immediately toward the library. We passed empty classrooms and passed through silent halls. I could barely see through the dark, but I had this school memorized like the back of my hand. We had no issue at all navigating our way in the dark.

When we got to the library doors, Nathaniel retrieved another key and unlocked it while I held the flashlight.

I heard the sound of footsteps down the hall, sending my heartrate skyrocketing. Both our heads ripped that direction and we saw the approaching halo of a flashlight.

We slipped inside and silently helped the door close. Nathaniel clicked the lock back into place, and we quietly backed away from the door.

We stared at it, holding our breath.

The footsteps hesitated just outside the door.

I thought my heart was going to explode.

I'd get expelled.

My father would be disgraced if his daughter was caught sneaking around the school after hours, with a boy.

Nathaniel would lose his scholarship.

But soon the footsteps resumed and kept walking down the hall.

I let out a sharp breath, my heart beginning to calm.

Nathaniel looked over at me, and I saw how I felt on his face.

He extended a hand to me, and together, we cut through the study area toward the back of the library.

The McCallum room was one at the very back of the library, on the south side. It was an area I rarely went to. With the flashlight on, we walked down the hall, and there, up ahead, my eyes fixed on the door.

The doors to the rooms were never closed unless someone was studying in them. So, they were wide open when we got there.

This room was little more than a nook. There was one single chair pushed in the corner to the left, and there wasn't much room for anything else. But the shelves were packed, packed as tight as they could be.

"Let me see that," Nathaniel said, reaching for the flashlight. I handed it over, and he looked down at the card. And then he shined the light on the spines of the books, looking for the number.

First, he scanned the left side of the shelves. And then he looped to the shelves straight ahead from the door. Down one shelf, and then the next.

And then he paused, about a third of the way down the next shelf. The light moved slightly from one book to the next.

"I was right," he said. "This number doesn't even exist. The book for this card should be right here."

I stepped forward and looked at the number on the

card and then the numbers on the shelf. It skipped from one to the next.

Something sparked in the back of my mind. I reached forward and grabbed the two books to the right and the left of the non-existent book. I pulled them from the shelf.

And there, in the backing of the bookshelf, was a lock.

CHAPTER ELEVEN

I darted forward and started digging through the bag around Nathaniel's chest. My fingers fumbled around the candles and the matches, and finally, they gripped the cold metal of the key. I drew it out, and the room was utterly silent as Nathaniel and I stared at it.

My hands shook just a little as I reached for the lock.

All the air in my lungs left my body when I slipped it into the lock, and it fit.

I twisted the key, and there was a click.

Immediately, the entire bookcase popped out toward us, just a little.

I caught Nathaniel's eyes for just a moment. His

gaze perfectly reflected the wonder and fear and excitement I felt inside.

He gripped the edge of a shelf and pulled back.

The whole thing swung open with little trouble, hinging back toward us. We stepped to the side, and Nathaniel shined the light behind it.

It was a small space. Maybe six feet by six feet. Two other bookshelves lined the walls on either side, though they were only maybe half filled.

There was a window straight across, and to my surprise, it wasn't boarded off or blacked out.

And right in the middle of the space, there was an intricate, metal, spiral staircase that rose up.

I didn't hesitate a second. I grabbed the flashlight from Nathaniel and started up the stairs.

I wound up and up. The ceilings in the library were tall. I had always assumed there were classrooms on the second floor above the private rooms of the library. But this was a secret door and a hidden staircase.

There was no door at the top of the stairs. It simply stepped out into a room.

And tears instantly pricked my eyes the second I took one breath.

It smelled exactly like my mother.

As I shone the light around the space, I saw her in every inch of it. There was a desk in the very middle and on it there were pages full of her handwriting.

There was a vase of long dried daisies. My father brought them for her every Monday when they were blooming in our window boxes.

There were bookshelves wrapping around all the walls, except for where the window was. Though they were mostly empty. There was a bench below the window, and on the dusty cushion, lay one of her sweaters. A macramé swing was hung in one corner. There was a trash can in one corner, half full of food things. She always worked while she ate.

I couldn't stand any more. I sank back and crouched, wrapping my arms around my shins. Tears immediately welled in my eyes and started rolling down my cheeks. I pressed my lips together, holding it all in.

Nathaniel knelt beside me, wrapping an arm around my shoulders.

I looked around, and I could see pieces of my mother in every corner of this hidden office. I could smell her just like she was here, herself. If I closed my eyes, I could swear she was here.

"We'll find your answers, Margot," Nathaniel said, rubbing his hand up and down my arm. "We'll figure out what happened to your mother."

I nodded my head, but I was still holding my breath. When I realized, I sucked in a sharp one and wiped the tears from my face. I took three deep breaths, in and out. I told myself that I could do this. I could do it for her. I could do it for my dad. And I could do it for me.

And Nathaniel, because he was a part of everything, too.

Nathaniel pulled me back up to my feet and waited for my cue. Cautiously, I stepped forward toward the closest bookshelf. Really, it was strange how few books were on the shelves. At the far side of the room, I saw a dozen boxes that looked filled to the brim with books.

My father said she'd been collecting more and more books. I wondered what my mother's organization was. Why were some on the shelves, and some in the boxes?

I reached for one of the books on the shelves. I opened it to somewhere in the middle.

I thought it was in German. I didn't know anything besides English and Latin. But I understood enough to immediately recognize the word *hexe*.

Witch.

I extended it out to Nathaniel, who took it and started looking over the words.

"My German is still terrible," he said. "But I think this is an account of family history. Of the witches in the Kroger family being hunted."

He looked up at me and there was a spark in his eyes.

There was wonder and hope.

I walked a little further down the shelf and pulled another book off.

This was a journal. The dates read 1699. I would have to search the entire thing for what we were looking for. But at the very end, it was signed by Tavin McGregor. Mare's son.

We divided. Nathaniel and I went in opposite directions, pulling out books and scanning. Though in reality, there were only about 30 books on the shelves.

It wasn't always obvious, what the books were about. Some seemed like they were fairy tales, or just regular history. Some were obvious instruction books. But as we'd learned, not everything could be taken at its face value.

Nathaniel called me over and I looked down at the thin book he held. He laid it flat on the desk, and then touched the pages. He looked over at me, and then I did the same.

It changed from some language that had no Latin origins, to something I could easily read.

Just like the book of telekinesis.

It was a book about glamouring.

I stood up, and my heart pounded.

This was it. This was what we had been looking for. What we needed to learn…everything. Anything.

We'd had nothing.

But my mother must have spent years collecting and learning.

"How long did she know?" I asked aloud as I turned and looked around. I realized then, the books in the boxes weren't anything. They were nothing. False leads and hope. My mother had gone through hundreds, maybe thousands of books, looking for anything to do with being a mage. This curation didn't happen overnight. "This...she had to have known for years. Why...why didn't she ever say anything?"

Nathaniel looked around. He reached for another book, another journal. "She knew a lot more than we do, obviously. She was a historian. She knew how many people were killed over the centuries. She knew the danger."

And for the first time, it hit me personally. That there really were people killed for being able to do the same kinds of things Nathaniel and I could do.

Our abilities were dangerous.

They made us a target.

These were modern times, things were different.

But were they? When it came down to it, would the government, the military just look the other way if somehow either of us were exposed?

And for the first time, it dawned on me that something really, really bad could have happened to my mother because she was a mage. Someone could have hurt her. Taken her. Anything. Because she could do things that should have been impossible.

I wrapped my arms around my waist and told myself I couldn't let my imagination run away with itself. We had to handle this logically. We had to be diligent.

I crossed to the desk and sat down in Mom's chair. I scooted in and looked down at what she'd lain upon it.

There were two books stacked on each other. There were a dozen loose papers spread over the desk, each with her handwriting on them. Three seemed to be pages of notes about what I assumed was in those two books. Others were totally random notes. A stray thought, an appointment with the dentist. A school assignment of mine that I would need Mom's help with.

But to the left side of the desk, there was a book entirely filled with her handwriting. I pulled it closer and read the page it was left open to.

I traced the last English line, her writing read. *It dated up until 1701, and then the trail went cold. Months of letters and phone calls and assistance from the very kind people in England, and that was it. I can't find any evidence of magic users past that date. They all left for America or they died out. I think all traces of magic disappeared within years of when it did in America.*

I looked up at Nathaniel, who was leaning over my shoulder, reading along as I did.

"My mother was a linguist. That's what she taught. But she was also renowned as a historian," I said. "She never gave up. The discoveries she made…she could have traveled the world with archeologists. She knew how to do her research. I would believe every word she's written in this book."

Nathaniel reached forward and turned the page back and his eyes quickly scanned. My mother talked about trying to track down the last of a mage family from Germany. The trail had gone cold with the death of two people in 1692.

"I think I was right," he breathed. "I think all traces of magic disappeared right around 1700." He twisted and sat on the edge of the desk, his eyes distant as he thought. "One by one they were hunted into extinction." His voice grew far away, breathy. "But blood is almost impossible to squash. It was all just… forgotten, because the ancestors who knew what they were doing were killed. We've just lain…dormant, for centuries."

His eyes slid back over to mine, and I saw something big there. "I think there are more of us out there, Margot. Maybe not many. But you and I, we can't be the only ones. I don't know if anyone else has found what we have. I think it's up to us to resurrect magic."

My eyes cast around the office. There were books here, so many things to be learned. But this couldn't be the entirety of it. We were talking about the entire history of mankind.

I felt another shift then. In what my future would look like. I'd always had it mapped out. I'd had it planned.

I would become a professor, like my parents. I would marry a nice man. I would have my own children. I would live a simple but happy life.

But I felt all of that change. I felt it get bigger. I felt it get darker. I felt it get a lot harder.

I was the descendant of witches. I had powers. Abilities. I wasn't normal. I wasn't simple.

As I looked around my mother's office, I felt it. This was my heritage. My mother's legacy.

This was something big that I knew I could do with my life.

And I wanted it.

I suddenly wanted it more than I'd ever wanted anything.

"We have a lot of reading to do," I said, giddy with the possibility of it.

CHAPTER TWELVE

The coming weeks seemed to pass by in a blink.

Nathaniel and I spent three days going through the books on the shelves. There were twenty-eight of them. Four were journals. Nine were historical books. Nine seemed to be some kind of instructional books. And six we could not categorize.

We went through my mother's desk, searching for anything and everything. What we found were more books and more notes and things we didn't understand yet.

But before we went through my mother's journal, we brought my dad here. His reaction to seeing the hidden office was much the same as mine. He'd cried.

He'd taken a solid five minutes just to take it in. He'd had to sit down.

But I saw something like peace in his eyes when he took it all in. I saw something lift off of his shoulders.

He knew he hadn't done anything to her, despite what the police had believed for a while. But he had always wondered if he'd made her unhappy. If she hadn't been content with her life.

Now he had more closure. Now he knew.

It was nothing to do with us. It had everything to do with the magic she had discovered.

I believed it. Nathaniel believed it. And now I thought my father believed it.

And together, we read through my mother's notes.

This book was concerned with the history of magic, which surprised no one. She'd traced every person who was killed at the Salem Witch Trials. Only Mare and one other had been true mages, so far as she could find. She'd gone back through her lineage and picked out the others. She'd done endless research.

She studied the witch hunts of Germany, Scotland, England, Denmark.

Her conclusion was that there was a surge of magical ability that began around 1500. That the knowledge of the mages had been shared, that their study had been furthered. She believed they grew more confident in what they could do.

And in the end, it got them killed.

The witch hunts got intense and were widespread throughout the world between 1536 and 1693.

After that timeframe, she couldn't find any evidence of magic users.

She too thought the mages had been hunted into oblivion. She thought we were the descendants of those motherless and fatherless children who were never able to teach their children what they could do.

It was overwhelming and heartbreaking. So many lives had been lost. So much knowledge was now lost to the world.

We didn't notice it at first, but as we sorted through the twenty-eight books, we found there was a note written on the inside cover of each of them. It was written in my mother's handwriting. And it described where she'd found each one.

Three were from the Salem Public Archives.

Two were from the Boston Public Library.

Two from Alderidge University.

And the rest were from singular locations.

We thought we'd discovered all my mother's secrets. Until my father bumped into her desk, and from a shelf inside the top of one of the drawers, another book fell out.

When we pulled it out, my eyes stung for just a

moment. It was her personal journal. A record of her personal experiences as a mage.

We stayed up the entire night reading it.

Mom had found a book in the library of the professor who she replaced. It was a book of stories. It talked about turning water into wine. It told stories about turning rags into beautiful garments. Old tall tales. But she recorded that when she touched it, a golden shimmer washed over the book. She felt something different.

So she tried it, thinking it was silly.

But it worked.

She found another book while we'd been on a weekend to Boston. In the public library. It had revealed itself to her by whispering to her as she passed by. She didn't give many more details about what that meant.

But over the course of four years, she amassed this collection of books. And she was able to do all the things the books taught her.

Her abilities slowly grew stronger. She recorded her guilt for not telling my father, but she was afraid. Not of him. But of what sharing her secret might invite. There could be dire consequences. He could get hurt. She could be hunted.

And I'd cried when I came to the passage toward

the end, where my mother said she'd tested me when I was fourteen. And she knew what I was.

She was going to tell me when I turned eighteen. She would teach me.

I was nineteen now. I could have known for over a year. I could have been learning this whole time.

The last entry in her journal dated just two days before she disappeared. She talked about two books she'd bought from a dealer in England. They'd taken two months just to be shipped across the ocean and arrive at her office. She hadn't had a chance to look through them yet, but they looked like they contained new information.

And there was nothing else after that.

I wished she were still here. If she could accomplish all of this on her own, what might we accomplish with the three of us? How much could we further this? How much more might we find?

So, over the coming weeks, Nathaniel and I started going through the books. We still had our lives to balance, school schedules and homework and work at the library. But with very little sleep, we were managing to read nearly a book a day.

And we spent every single hour we weren't in class or at the library, together. We nearly lived together, and to my surprise, my father didn't stop us. Nathaniel came over to our house half of the nights and ended up sleeping on the couch, or I went to the solarium and now my father knew where I was the nights I didn't come home.

We didn't always talk much when we were together. It was hours spent curled up together on a bed, our heads bent over books. It was me lying in his lap, him with one arm propped up along the back of the couch, a book in his other hand.

"We need somewhere safe to practice," I said one chilly evening at the end of October. "It's a risk doing it here." I looked around the solarium, where we'd been attempting to make an empty glass jar transform into a pencil. We were working on the book about transfiguration, and it was exceptionally challenging. "You're always at risk of being caught here. Anyone could wander by and see that you're living here. Your walls are literally made of glass. Someone could easily walk past and see what we're doing."

Nathaniel sat on his bed, holding one ankle, the other foot flat on the floor. I watched him wrack his brain. And then a light sparked in his eyes. "Come on," he said as he stood. He held a hand out for me and scooped up the book on the coffee table. "I have an idea."

I pulled on my coat, as did he. We gathered up the supplies we were using, and together we walked out into the fast approaching winter.

There was a shortcut to the beach through the forgotten garden. Hand in hand, Nathaniel led me down the stone path, through the thick bushes that had lost their leaves. We had to walk carefully to avoid being caught by the thorns. I was about to suggest we prune them back, but I shut my mouth. If the path looked taken care of, someone might get curious and come looking.

We stepped out onto the beach, and Nathaniel pointed us south.

The tide was low, so thankfully the sand was dry. There was little seaweed up on shore, and even now, there was very little driftwood. The beach was surprisingly clean and pristine.

It was also entirely empty, because it was only forty degrees and the wind was blowing strong.

But as soon as we started walking, I knew exactly where we were headed.

It took ten minutes, because walking in sand wasn't the easiest, but we finally got to the stone steps and made our way up the bank.

Asteria House sat there, just as forlorn and decrepit as the last time Nathaniel and I came here.

"Grab some of this wood," I said, nodding my chin at the broken twigs and branches that were tangled into the bushes around us. "There's a fireplace in there. Let's see if we can't get some warmth inside."

We gathered up as much as we could carry, and then walked inside.

If anything, it felt colder inside than it did outside. It smelled musky in here, and it was dark with no lights on. I squatted next to the fireplace and set to propping up all the kindling, while Nathaniel walked around the house and closed all the windows.

I closed my eyes for a moment when I was done and tried to recall the words I'd read. I'd only briefly glanced through them as we sorted through the books.

I brought my hands together and rubbed them quickly, creating heat. I opened my eyes, looking at the kindling. And then I snapped my fingers.

Fire instantly leapt to life in the kindling.

"Where did you learn that one?"

I startled at Nathaniel's voice behind me. I twisted around to see him blowing into his hands in an attempt to warm them.

"It was in one of the books from Mom's office," I said as I stood, watching the flames grow brighter and hotter. "I can't remember which one. I read it while we were sorting through everything."

I clung my arms to myself, trying to keep warm. Nathaniel pulled me into his arms, wrapping them around me and hugging me tightly into his chest. He wasn't any warmer than I was, but I lay my head against his chest and breathed in peacefully.

Quietly, we watched the fire grow. Slowly, the air grew warmer.

Nathaniel started humming a soft song. It was something I didn't recognize. But he took my right hand in his left. He held it light and gentle. And he wrapped his right hand around my lower back. And gently, he swayed us to the music he hummed. Back and forth. No pressure. No time limits. Just me and him.

I looked up at his face, staring into his green eyes. My heart felt at peace. I felt relaxed.

I wasn't stressing about how much we had to learn. I wasn't trying to figure out how to balance this with my class load.

I was just there, with him.

When he came to the end of his song, he leaned forward and pressed his lips to mine. My hands slid up to the back of his neck, pulling him closer to me. His hands came to my lower back.

This felt so natural. It just felt…good. Like it was something that I'd done every day for my entire life. It felt like something we could do every day for the rest of our lives.

He looked into my eyes when he released me, and I smiled.

"What would you do with this house if it were

yours?" I asked, turning away. I kept one of his hands in mine, and looked around the massive room.

Nathaniel cast his eyes around and chuckled. "Hope and pray I somehow magically came into a lot of money."

He was right. It would take some money to get this place back to livable conditions. All the windows facing the ocean side were cracked or broken. Most of the siding was destroyed on that side, as well.

And with the windows blown out, water had gotten inside and caused significant damage to the walls and especially the floors.

The kitchen had been destroyed by looters. There was evidence of homeless people having lived upstairs at one point.

It was a mess.

But it wouldn't be impossible to bring back.

With the right amount of money.

Nathaniel's words sparked an idea. An impossible one, for now, but an idea.

"I'd want a great big couch here," I said, stepping into the middle of the room and indicating my hands along one space. "And a huge rug in the middle. A really thick one, thick enough you could sleep on it."

I turned and walked to the grand dining room. It was one of the only things that hadn't been looted, the chandelier that hung above it, because no one could reach it. Great big windows looked out over the ocean. "And a huge dining table here, big enough to fit fifteen people."

Nathaniel chuckled again, following me through the house. "Just how many children are you planning on having, Margot?"

Instantly, I felt my face blush and from the look in Nathaniel's eyes, I saw that he realized what he'd just said. He looked embarrassed, but I could also tell he was truly thinking about it.

I fixed my gaze on him as I slowly walked toward him and then wrapped my arms around his waist. "A whole brood," I said, smiling. "With seven boys and five girls."

Nathaniel raised an eyebrow at me as he wrapped his arms around my waist. "You want twelve children?"

I laughed, tipping up and kissing him soft and gentle. "Fine," I said, teasing. "I'll settle for two boys and three girls."

He just smiled and kissed me again, and I knew that nothing about the future was certain. Anything could happen and anything could change.

But something right here felt real. It felt like a promise.

Here we were talking about having five children when we'd never even said I love you, and we'd never even had sex yet.

But still, I turned, pulling Nathaniel after me as I walked into the kitchen and talked about the cabinets I'd install, and the double oven and the pantry big enough to store food for an entire year.

Room after room, Nathaniel followed behind me while I daydreamed about living in a mansion like this with a whole flock of children. And the further we explored, the more we realized that even five children would never fill all the rooms. There had to be somewhere around fifteen bedrooms, and a dozen bathrooms.

Finally, we returned from our renovation tour to the grand living room. Nathaniel spun me in a dance spin and dipped me low. My hair hung behind me, sweeping to the floor. I smiled up at him, and I realized then just how much I loved his smile. I loved how he was when it was just the two of us. I loved the man he showed me when it was just me and him.

"Never stop smiling at me, Margot," Nathaniel said as he slowly stood me back up. He placed a hand along my jaw, caressing my face. And there was something a little sad in his eyes. There was something that spoke to his terrible childhood, and I had to wonder. How many smiles were ever pointed in his direction? How many tender words were spoken to him? Who had ever cared for him in his life?

I reached up, mirroring his position, and gently kissed his lips. "Never," I promised him.

And as difficult as it was, we pulled away from each other's arms. We pulled out the book and the supplies. And we worked. We did the hand motions. We concentrated. And after an hour of trying, we turned a glass jar into a pencil.

CHAPTER THIRTEEN

HALLOWEEN CAME AND WENT. CLASSES STARTED heating up and there were beginning to be signs of students breaking down. This first semester was when you could start to tell if a student was going to make it all the way or not. Dad always said he knew by October if a student was going to drop out or not.

November brought with it bitterly cold wind. Which made working in Asteria House difficult. We tried bringing every spare blanket and set of sheets we could find and boarded them over the windows, attempting to insulate from the wind. But on the days there was sideways rain, we resorted to sneaking into my mother's hidden office to practice.

And I started having to study for classes as we got further into the meat of the semester.

Nathaniel and I found time to get together each day, but our *us* time grew less and less. Our classes were intense, especially Nathaniel's, considering he was a junior. But we were both focused on the future, not this short term. We did what we had to do.

But I started reevaluating my goals.

What did I really want to do with my future? Was being a Latin professor really what I wanted now? Was a life at Alderidge really the best thing I could do with myself, considering the new things I had learned?

I wouldn't voice those thoughts to Nathaniel. He was so close now. After this, he only had three more semesters and he would be done with his undergraduate. At least then he could decide if more education was what he still wanted.

So, we went about our days, studying until our eyes were tired and our brains felt ready to explode from having to store so much information.

The middle of November, I walked hand in hand down the hall with Nathaniel. I was finished with classes, Thursday being one of my lighter days. But Nathaniel had two more classes. I walked him to his next class, discussing if either of us thought the potions book from my mother's library was plausible or not. We both had doubts.

"You're coming over for dinner tonight, right?" I

asked, stopping outside his classroom and leaning in the door. "Dad's making lasagna."

"I wouldn't miss it," he said, leaning down and pressing a kiss to my lips with a smile.

I bit my lower lip and watched as he walked away into the room.

I appreciated his shoulders. The lean muscles in his forearms. His narrow hips. The set of his jaw, and the pout of his lips.

With a smile, I turned out from the door and headed down the hall.

I was halfway down it when someone fell into step beside me.

I looked over to see David Sinclair.

I didn't even try to resist rolling my eyes.

"I brought you something," he said, leaning in, a sly smile on his face. He extended a package out to me.

It was a small box with a big white bow attached to the lid. I gave him a doubtful side glance as I opened it.

Displayed inside was a beautiful set of diamond earrings, larger than any center piece I'd seen on any wedding ring.

"What's this about?" I ask, looking straight forward down the hall. "Why?"

"Because beautiful, smart, powerful women should have beautiful presents," David said. He walked a little closer, his shoulder brushing against mine.

I stopped dead in my tracks, only I wished I had kept walking when I looked down the hall and saw David's lackies following behind. All of them. Borden, James, Donald, Gerald, and Howard.

"Do you have amnesia, David?" I asked.

He blinked at me. "No. Why?"

"Because I know I told you quite clearly a few weeks ago that I'm not interested," I said. I handed the box back to him and he took it with a disappointed and confused expression. "You and I are never going to be an option."

"But *Nathaniel Nightingale* is the kind of man you're into?" he asked doubtfully.

I didn't much like the look on his face.

"Nathaniel is exactly the kind of man I'm into," I said, taking a step forward. Borden and James stepped forward, coming to David's side like they were going to protect him from me. I smiled, looking all three of them up and down. "Because he never needed to corner me with back-up to protect his feelings from being hurt."

Borden's hand darted forward and clasped around my upper arm, his fingers digging in hard.

I looked down at it, a look of disgust curling on my face.

I called out to the dirt beneath his fingernails and asked it to shove back beneath them.

He let go of me with a hiss, shaking his hand out. With confusion, he glared at me, but he didn't say anything.

David glowered at Borden, and I at least had to give him that. He hadn't liked that Borden had put his hands on me.

"Stop asking me out," I said, looking back at David. "I'm with Nathaniel. I'm exceptionally happy. And you and I are never going to happen."

And with that, I turned on my heel, and I walked away.

ONE WEEK LATER, I was headed to my writing class, when I spotted Borden and James talking to Nathaniel in the hall. Heat instantly flared in my veins. Because they weren't really talking. Nathaniel's back was against a wall and the both of them were right in his face.

I stormed down the hall. My hands curled into fists and I felt heat gathering there.

I was still learning what I was doing. But I knew my hands were growing hot enough that if I were to touch, or slap, or punch either of them, they'd be severely burned.

But when I was halfway to them, Borden looked over. His eyes widened just a bit. He nudged James in the shoulder, who looked over his shoulder and found me in the hall.

Trying to look cool and calm, they both walked away from Nathaniel.

I walked right past Nathaniel, determined that I was going to put an end to this, for good, when Nathaniel's hand snapped out, grabbing my wrist. Had he been anything but a mage, he probably would have been burned from the temperature of my skin.

"Don't, Margot," he breathed out. "It's not worth it."

Maybe I was still too angry. Maybe I was flaring too hot. But I stopped in my tracks and my head whipped back to look at Nathaniel.

"Why won't you stand up to them?" I seethed. "Why won't you make them stop, even if it means a few bruises once? Why won't you tell David how it is so he will finally leave us alone?"

Shocked hurt reflected in his face. There was something in his eyes, and if I'd taken a moment, maybe I would have been able to read it.

But I was too angry. At him. At the Society Boys. At life.

So, I just turned, and I stormed off in the opposite direction, headed to my last stupid class of the day.

. . .

I AVOIDED Nathaniel for the rest of the day. I regretted what I'd said. I didn't buy into society's expectation of manliness. I didn't want Nathaniel to feel as if he had to be macho and swing his fists and grunt and claim *woman, mine.*

I just wanted him to stand up for himself.

I wanted him to make them stop.

Because I knew what he was capable of. I knew the power he possessed. I knew he could do terrible things to them.

Not only that, but he was a far better person than them.

He was kind and smart and clever.

I would fight for him.

But I wanted him to fight by my side.

So that night, I quietly sat at dinner with Dad, just the two of us. He asked me repeatedly if something was wrong. I told him that I just needed to think through some things. So, he changed the subject and asked about our progress with learning magic. I didn't mind telling him about that. We talked about fire-starting and transforming. We talked about history and the few details he'd managed to dig up about a witch hunt in Indonesia.

My father couldn't really help with resurrecting magic.

But he could be there for me to help me process everything I had to handle. He could be an outlet, and that was exactly what I needed then. A distraction.

I went to bed that night, only to stare up at the ceiling for two hours.

CHAPTER FOURTEEN

Maybe Nathaniel understood me better than I gave him credit for.

He gave me my space over the next six days. He didn't push me. He didn't try to apologize. He let me deal with my thoughts, and I assumed he was doing the same.

We passed each other in the halls. We gave side glances in the library.

But we didn't seek each other out.

Unfortunately, that meant David and the Society Boys thought they saw an opportunity.

One day a bouquet of flowers was waiting on my desk when I arrived in Latin.

There was a box of fancy chocolates from Paris on my desk during Writing another day.

I found an expensive purse and custom stationary on my doorstep one night.

None of them had a note or a name from the sender. But it was no question who they came from, which is exactly why he didn't claim them.

David saw that Nathaniel and I were on rocky ground and was taking his opportunity.

When we both walked into the school at the same time, David held the door open for me. When I walked from one building to the other for my class, he held an umbrella over my head to shield me from the rain.

He even started talking to my father in the halls, laughing and making jokes.

I never said one word. I never acknowledged his presence.

But he persisted.

How did he know? He said he could tell I was a powerful woman. But how could he really know that? Because I'd stood up to him? Because I wasn't scared of him and his Society Boys?

I *was* a powerful woman.

I had incredible potential.

But he had no idea what kind.

So why me? Why was he so fixated on having me by his side?

As the days stretched on, my heart started to hurt

when I walked down the halls and my eyes met Nathaniel's.

We hadn't solved any of our problems. Nathaniel and I were both stubborn. We were both who we were. Was either of us ever going to get over this and make things right?

Until something clicked, until one of us figured out how to change something, we were stuck.

We were in a bad place, but I couldn't stand the thought of him being alone for Thanksgiving. He didn't have a family. The day would come, and he would be sitting alone in his solarium, eating some cheap meal out of a container.

Sometimes, I could be a big person.

So, when school was over, I walked down the hall to wait a few minutes until he was out of his French class. Five minutes passed. And of course, while I waited, I saw David walking down the hall toward me.

"Big plans for Thanksgiving break?" he asked. He leaned up against the wall, mirroring my position. To his credit, he left a two-foot gap between us.

"Just staying home with my dad," I said, refusing to look at him.

"Your father's a fascinating man," David said. "I could talk to my father, see if he could get him on the board at the Boston Public. He knows how to open all the doors."

"My father's quite happy teaching," I said, the temperature of my blood rising slightly.

"Just an offer," David said. "I'm here to help, Margot. Anything you need."

Finally, I did look over at him, just so I could glare.

He met my gaze, and just smiled. "We're headed up to the Vermont house for Thanksgiving. I'm going to miss your beautiful face. Maybe next year you'll be coming with me."

My mouth opened to say something nasty, but just then the door opened, and students came out of the classroom, led by Nathaniel.

I wanted to rip all of David's teeth out, one by one, when he got a smug smile on his lips and looked from Nathaniel, back to me. He pushed off the wall and held my gaze as he walked down the hall.

I glared at him, resisting the temptation to light his coat on fire. I could do it. But it might cause a scene.

Nathaniel stepped forward but couldn't quite meet my eyes. Everything about his body language screamed doubt and worry.

I wanted to make him feel better.

But I was still angry that all of this was going on and he still wouldn't stand up for himself or us.

"Thanksgiving is in two days," I said. Even though he wouldn't fully look at me, I fixed him hard with my gaze. And everything in me ached for him. I wanted to touch him. I wanted him to touch me. I wanted his tongue in my mouth and his air filling my lungs. "I can't stand the thought of you being alone. So, you're coming to my house. I don't care if things are hard and weird. I'm going to be really angry if you don't show up. So be there. Five o'clock."

Finally, his eyes rose up to mine. I saw a nervous boy there. But I saw a spark.

I didn't know what it meant. I was too angry and confused to evaluate it.

So, I turned on my heel, and I walked away.

CHAPTER FIFTEEN

I was nervous.

It was Thanksgiving Day and Dad and I were in the throes of getting everything ready. And I knew. I just knew that Nathaniel wouldn't show up at the last second to eat.

As I'd expected, there was a knock on the door an hour and a half early. I let Dad go get it. He knew Nathaniel was coming over. They chatted and seemed happy to see each other. And I didn't look up as they came into the kitchen.

Dad put Nathaniel to work on the potatoes and then the glazed carrots. I kept working on the rolls and the cranberry sauce.

And then at five o'clock, we sat down together at the table. Dad said grace and we dished up our food.

Dad made easy conversation, talking about the coming weeks with finals and preparations for Christmas. He even eventually dragged Nathaniel and me into a gratitude monologue. I said I was grateful for a warm home. Nathaniel said he was grateful for education.

And we almost made it through without anything dramatic happening.

But I got down to my last four bites. And then Dad pounded his fists on the table, not hard, but hard enough, a knife curled into one hand, his fork in the other.

"Alright, you two," Dad said, fixing us with a serious look. "I know neither of you wants to talk about what happened. But this is dragging on long enough. I'm getting tired of you both being so miserable."

I looked up with wide eyes, and my heart instantly started beating hard.

He was going to go there.

He was going to drag us all through the mud.

"I've seen both versions of Nathaniel and Margot and this latter version is ridiculous," Dad continued. Nathaniel's eyes slid over to meet mine and I stared at him, his expression serious. "I know I'm supposed to be all protective of my daughter and give any man interested in her a hard time, but I've never seen two people who were more made for each other. So, I want you both to go upstairs and hash it all out, no matter how loud or ugly it gets, and get this over with. Relationships are hard. So be grown-ups, and work through this."

Dad leaned back in his seat and set to cutting into a piece of turkey. He kept his eyes down and chewed on his bite with vigor like he hadn't just reamed us both.

Nathaniel and I looked at each other, sitting there ramrod straight.

"Now, please," Dad said, a bit of a sharp edge to his voice.

I blinked twice, shocked at my father's abrupt attitude.

But I pushed my chair back, as did Nathaniel. And silently and awkwardly, we left the dining room. He followed me up the stairs. My hands grew slick with sweat as I reached for my doorknob. My heart was racing.

We stepped inside, and I closed the door behind us.

I walked to the window, my arms folded over my chest. I stared out at the snow that was beginning to fall softly on the school grounds.

"I don't want it to be like this between us," I said, stating it as a fact, in case he didn't realize.

Nathaniel didn't say anything, and I really wanted

him to say something. I looked back at him, and I knew it for sure, that I was glaring.

"David Sinclair has been pursuing me hard. He's a shark and he smells my blood in the water," I said. Nathaniel was looking at the books on my shelf, lined up in no organized manner. "He thinks we'd be a good match."

"And what do you think, Margot?" he asked. Finally, his eyes at least met mine.

"I think he's an arrogant asshole," I said as the temperature of my blood rose a few degrees. "I think he's used to getting what he wants, and this is turning into a game to him. He saw an opportunity because everything is all messed up between us, and he thinks he's going to wear me down."

"Is he right?" Nathaniel asked.

The heat in me flared. I took a step forward and I shoved Nathaniel a little. "No, he's not right. Because I'm just heart broken and waiting. But I can appreciate that he's not hesitating. That he's going after what he wants. Nathaniel, I just…" I turned away from him, my hands rising into my hair.

I faced the wall, but I wasn't seeing anything. I was replaying every scene between Nathaniel and the Society Boys.

"You could literally kill any of them by hardly lifting a finger," I said with my back turned to him.

"You're capable of so much. And you let them walk all over you."

"We are good together, Margot," Nathaniel's words slipped from him in a breath. They wrapped their way around my entire body, and I was instantly ensnared by them. "But you don't know everything about me. You'll never fully understand where I come from, Margot, not one hundred percent. You don't know that all the times I did stand up for myself, all the fights I got myself into, all the times it landed me in juvenile detention, and it didn't get me anything."

I started to understand the scars covering his body. The ones I'd seen on his back. The ones I could clearly see across his knuckles, the one just over his left eyebrow.

"I *can* defend myself, Margot," he said. He raised his hands up and let his hands curl into fists. And there, I saw the white scars stand out even sharper. His hands were covered in scars. "I could beat all of them to a bloody pulp. I once took on three boys who were four years older than me, because they were picking on me, and landed us all in the emergency room. When I was twelve, I got into a fight with a seventeen-year-old. We beat each other within an inch of our lives. I had to have a blood transfusion because I lost so much. I spent two years in juvenile detention. I learned ways to survive in there that you couldn't even imagine."

My heart was racing, and it jumped all the way into my throat when he pulled his shirt up and over his head. He let it drop to the ground.

His hand rose to a thick scar just under his right pectoral. "You'd be shocked what can be done with a toothbrush." His eyes rose to meet mine. "And I stabbed the other guy four times with my spoon before the guards could pull me off of him."

My eyes widened and my blood went colder as I pictured it all. Nathaniel fighting, every day of his life as he grew up. I imagine the violence in the group homes. The police he must have dealt with. The things he had to learn when he was locked up to defend himself.

"I got into a fight my junior year of high school," Nathaniel said. "I'd been trying to stay out of trouble that year. But some guys wouldn't leave me alone about being foster trash. I lost my cool. And it didn't go beyond fists and a couple of stitches. But my school counselor came to me and told me if I screwed up one more time I would be tried as an adult. Next time, it would be hard prison time with a longer sentence. And I'd never get out of the system."

I couldn't stop looking at him, in an entirely new light. There were dozens of scars over his whole body. Before, I'd thought he'd been the victim of abuse. And he had been. But it had also taught him to fight for his life.

Nathaniel could defend himself against the Society Boys. But at what cost?

"So, I vowed to stop it all," Nathaniel continued. I saw something haunted in his eyes then. I saw his past. I saw the pain, but I also saw the anger he'd let control and protect him for so long. "I focused on school. I kept my head low. I took a few blows. And I worked my ass off to bring my grades up to perfection so I could get out."

He took a step forward, but we were still half a room apart. "I won't fight David and his boys because I don't know what will happen if I open that door again. I don't know who I'll be. I'm sorry it makes you angry, and I'm sorry if I'm disappointing you, but if that's the kind of man you want me to be again, Margot, I just won't do it."

Emotions pricked the back of my eyes. My lower lip trembled a little bit. I was angry. I was angry at myself for not understanding. I was angry for the way I was acting.

I took a step forward, and gently, I brought my fingers up to touch one of the scars that ran across his chest.

"I'm sorry," I said, and the words trembled just as much as my lip did. "I'm sorry I was disappointed and angry with you. And I'm sorry David keeps picking on you."

I stared at his chest, because I had a hard time meeting his eyes then.

"But *I* can't just stand there and take their shit," I said. And then I did look up at him. "I have a temper of my own and I can't stand bullies. So, when they act like they do, I can't not say anything."

I took a steadying breath, and I held Nathaniel's eyes. "I understand now, why you couldn't do what I wanted. And I'll never ask you to be different than you are again. But I also need you to not try and stop me when I need to call them out on their shit. When I might need to get into fights of my own."

Something lightened in Nathaniel's eyes then. He lifted a hand and covered mine with his, pressing my palm into his bare chest.

"So, we're in agreement?" he asked. I liked the way his chest rumbled with his words. "You won't get angry when I don't react to the Society Boys, because I don't want to kill any of them? And I won't try and stop you when you need to put them in their place?"

I took half a step closer and I couldn't resist when my eyes fell to his lips. "Exactly," I said softly as I nodded.

"I can handle that," he said, his words getting

quieter. His other hand rose to lace his fingers into my hair.

"Deal," I said.

And neither of us waited one moment longer. Our lips were on each other in the next breath.

The kiss was desperate. We'd both been starving and withering away for weeks now. We needed each other like we needed air, like we needed water. My hand rose all the way up his bare chest, which ignited a string of fireworks all down my body. My hand rose up into his hair, which had grown longer and a little wilder in the past few weeks.

I smiled a little against his lips.

"What?" he asked, smiling as well.

I shook my head. "Nothing. I just happen to like your hair like this."

He smiled too, huffing a tiny little laugh into my mouth.

Greedily, his hands slid down to my hips and he lifted me clean off the ground. My legs wrapped around his waist, and everything in me screamed more, more, more. Like I weighed nothing at all, Nathaniel walked with me wound around his body to the bed before he tipped onto it, his body pressing mine down into the mattress.

My tongue sought his out. My neck extended, my head falling back as his lips moved to my jaw and then down to the hollow beneath my ear. My back arched as his hands ran down my leg. And I couldn't stop touching him. There was so much bare skin under my hands, and I couldn't get enough. I needed more, needed to feel him.

After weeks of deprivation, I was nearly insane with need.

"Margot," Nathaniel breathed into my mouth, even as his hips ground heavenly into mine. "I missed you so much. Never, ever again."

I nodded as his kiss trailed down to my collar bones. "Never."

My eyes drifted open. And I instantly froze.

Every single book in my bedroom was floating. And every bit of earth—flowers, specks of dirt, and my entire wood desk and nightstand—were lifted off the ground at least a foot.

A curse slipped from my mouth, and everything related to earth came crashing back down to the ground.

With Nathaniel's start, all the paper came back down too. About thirty books clattered back to their space.

The two of us shot straight up, staring around at my bedroom in bewildered wonder.

"What in Zeus' name?" my father's voice called as he ran up the stairs. He didn't even knock. He stepped through my bedroom door, looking around for the source of the noise, noting that everything was in slight disarray.

And then he looked at Nathaniel and me. In my bed, Nathaniel with no shirt.

"I might want you two to make up," he said, glaring a little darkly. "But I'm not exactly looking to become a grandfather just yet."

Instantly, Nathaniel climbed off the bed and scrambled to pull his shirt back on over his head. "My apologies, Professor Bell."

My dad just huffed a laugh. He shook his head. "Professor Bell. I think by this point you can call me Arthur."

I had to press my lips together, because I knew the smile on my face would be ridiculous. But Nathaniel did let a little smile form on his own lips. And he just nodded.

My father looked back at me, and even though I knew he didn't love finding us the way he did, he was pleased that we'd worked things out. "Door open the rest of the night? Might be a good idea?"

I just nodded.

"Sure thing," Nathaniel said.

My father just shook his head. "Pie in ten minutes."

He walked out, and Nathaniel looked back at me.

His face was red with embarrassment. I couldn't help the silent little laugh that shook my chest.

Nathaniel shook his head at me, but didn't say anything as he crossed the room back to me. He sat on the edge of the bed and leaned forward, brushing the hair out of my face.

"The stories we're going to have to tell someday," he said. I loved the low, intimate, confident tone to his voice.

I didn't say anything. But I raised a hand and cupped his jaw. And I leaned forward, pressing one soft kiss to his lips.

"I want to promise no more drama," Nathaniel said. "But I can't see the future. But I swear I'll just try harder. Talk more. Because I think this is worth it."

"Me too," I said, nodding, meaning it with everything in me. "No more judgement."

Nathaniel nodded. "There's something I've been wanting to ask you."

My heart gave a tiny flip before I squashed it. It was overreacting.

"Would you go to the Winter Social Ball with me?"

The smile that split my face was comical. I knew I was overthinking his "question."

I tossed my head back and laughed at myself. "Yes," I answered, wrapping my arms around him, shaking my head.

The Winter Social Ball was the school's one and only social event. It was thrown the weekend before finals. It was the university equivalent of high school prom. Everyone brought dates, and everyone dressed up. There was a big formal dinner and dancing and because it was at a university, a lot of connections were made those nights that carried into everyone's professional years.

I'd only ever helped set up. Non-college students weren't allowed.

But I'd seen the magic of the night, and I'd been dying to go since I was twelve.

I leaned back and looked into Nathaniel's green eyes.

I was glad the fight was over. We needed to be together. I needed to be with him, to fight for him. To learn together.

I leaned in, and I kissed him once more, because I could.

CHAPTER SIXTEEN

The following Tuesday morning, I was eating breakfast when there was a tap on the door. I opened it, and instantly, a paper airplane landed in my hands.

With a smile, I unfolded it.

Can I walk you to class this morning?

Yes, I wrote on the paper, and it took off into the air.

Quickly, I finished eating my breakfast before dashing back up the stairs to brush my teeth. I checked myself in the mirror, grateful that I'd woken up a few minutes early today and had taken some time on my hair and makeup. I sported a tight-fitting black turtleneck and a plaid skirt that rode shorter than it should, but made my rear end look pretty fantastic. I topped it all off with black socks that came all the way up to my knees.

I pulled my shoes on, grabbed my coat, and slung my bag over my shoulder, just as there was a definitive knock on the door.

I opened it and I loved every millisecond of Nathaniel's eyes scanning up and down my entire body.

He stepped over the threshold and wrapped a hand around my waist. He pulled my middle to his and leaned down to kiss me.

"I might just keep you here at the house all for myself today instead," he growled into my mouth.

"As much as I like that idea, I kind of want to rub us in everyone's face today," I said, nipping at his bottom lip. "And I can't be late for class."

He smiled against my lips, pressing one last kiss to them. And then we turned and headed out the door, locking it behind us.

The snow was falling softly, sticking to the grass, but not the sidewalks yet. Hand in hand, Nathaniel and I walked back to the University.

Heads turned our way the moment we walked through the door. I clung to Nathaniel like a needy girlfriend, looking up into his handsome face and beaming for all the world to see. As we stepped into the common room, I reached a hand up, placing it on his cheek. He bent down and gave me what I wanted.

He kissed me hard and deep. I felt his grip on my hip tighten, digging into my flesh. It scrunched my skirt up and maybe I was showing more than I should, but I didn't care.

Nathaniel's tongue slipped into my mouth and I smiled as I let him kiss me deeper, relishing every electric current raging through my body.

Someone cleared their throat and I remembered where we were.

Half the students in the common area were staring at us. Some eyes immediately darted away as we came up for air, but others just stared in either disgust or jealousy.

And there, leaned up against the far wall, was David Sinclair. He was flanked by Borden and Howard.

David glared at the two of us with a darkness I'd not yet seen on his face. I watched as his fingers curled into a fist.

He leaned over and whispered something to Borden.

I gave him a smirk, leaning into Nathaniel. He leaned down as if he were expecting a whisper.

Instead, I licked his neck and then bit his earlobe.

Nathaniel looked down at me with surprise, but

hunger sparked in his eyes, and a thin smile curled in the corners of his mouth.

We stepped forward, heading down the hall to my first class.

Just before we stepped out of sight of the common room, Nathaniel's hand slid down my waist, to my rear. He gave it a squeeze.

I could feel David's eyes on us. I knew Nathaniel did it to rile him up.

But it still sent a thrill zipping through my lower belly.

I DIDN'T HAVE any spare time. Truly, I didn't. Between classes and our mage studies, I felt like I barely had time to sleep.

But I got everything ready at five in the morning. While in the library, I slipped a note to Nathaniel. Excitement sparked through my entire body when his eyes found me. I just smiled and walked back out.

At nine o'clock, when the library was closing, I slipped back inside. I went to the McCallum room and inserted the key into the back of the bookcase. Glancing over my shoulder that no one was watching, I swung it open and slipped inside, leaving the key for Nathaniel.

I wound my way up the spiral staircase. I stepped out into my mother's office.

I'd filled the space with golden balloons and streamers. A carefully wrapped present waited on Mom's desk. I'd stayed awake most of the night before baking the cake. And now I lit the candles, all twenty-two of them.

And with perfect timing, I faintly heard the sound of the lock in the bookcase and then it swinging open. I listened to Nathaniel's footsteps rising up the spiral staircase as I picked up the cake.

His entire face lit up when he saw me standing there. I started singing the birthday song softly and slowly as I crossed the dark space to him. He watched me the entire time, his eyes shining with appreciation and wonder.

"Happy birthday, dear Nathaniel," I sang, even though I didn't have much of a singing voice. "Happy birthday to you."

Nathaniel smiled and blew out the candles. And then he leaned forward through the smoke, and pressed a long, lingering kiss to my lips.

"Thank you, Margot," he said, leaning back, his eyes fixed on mine. "I...I haven't celebrated my birthday in...well," he shook his head. "I don't even remember."

I dipped my finger in the frosting and tapped it to

his nose. "You're very welcome," I said, watching his smile as he wiped the frosting from the bridge of his nose and ate it. "No promises it will be the best tasting cake, but it's the thought that counts, right?"

Nathaniel took the cake and set it aside on the desk. His eyes grew intense and deep as he wrapped his hands around my waist, sliding to my lower back. "It counts for everything, Margot," he said. "You've become the most important person in my entire world. I've been on my own for so long, been in survival mode for my entire life. I can't even describe what a saving angel you are to me."

I looped my arms behind his head and shifted up onto my tip toes so that I could kiss him. His lips were soft and rough, needy and freeing. I took a breath in as we kissed, and I memorized every way he smelled, every way he tasted up against my lips.

His hands slid lower until they gripped my outer thighs. As my need grew more urgent, I climbed right up him and wrapped my legs around his waist. He turned, crossing a few steps over to the chair and sank onto it, me wrapped around him while we tried our very best to devour one another.

His lips trailed from my mouth, to my jaw, down my throat.

I sighed, loving every moment we got together, praying they could continue for the rest of our lives.

But as my eyes slid open, they landed on the package on the desk, and suddenly I couldn't wait a moment longer.

"Your present," I said, leaning over and grabbing it. My neck suddenly felt cold with the absence of his lips. But still, I smiled, and held the present between the two of us.

Nathaniel returned my smile before his eyes fell to the package and he took it. Carefully, he opened the wrapping, and I had to wonder how many presents he'd ever opened in his life. From his careful method, I didn't think it was many.

The object on top was a framed picture of myself. Maybe it was vain, and I found myself instantly blushing as he studied it.

"You don't have a single picture in the solarium," I said softly, suddenly wishing I could take it back.

Nathaniel studied it in silence for several long moments.

But I knew I hadn't made a mistake when he looked up at me, meeting my eyes. I saw wonder and appreciation and longing there.

He reached up a hand, lacing his long fingers into my hair, but he looked back down at the picture again.

"Thank you," he breathed softly.

I muttered a response, feeling overwhelmed by his reaction and gratitude.

He set the picture in our laps, since I was still sitting wrapped around him. And then he pulled out the next item.

It was a journal. Wrapped in black leather, it had over three hundred pages bound within.

"You're a historian," I said. "I think it's time you start recording your own history."

He flipped through the pages, and I could already imagine them filled with his elegant handwriting.

"Thank you, Margot," he said as he looked up at me. He leaned forward, pressing his lips gently to mine.

"You're welcome," I muttered against his lips as I got lost in them again.

CHAPTER SEVENTEEN

WINTER CAME IN FULL EFFECT. IN THE COMING weeks, we received nearly two feet of snow. Students were in full-fledged panic mode. Finals were quickly approaching. We were neck deep in studies. Classes were at their most intense.

I was learning to survive off only five hours of sleep. Because as soon as we were out of classes and Nathaniel wasn't working at the library, he and I were headed to Asteria House to study. Book after book, we worked. Some things we mastered. Others, we failed at miserably.

It was slow learning. We had to go through endless trial and error. We'd set things on fire. We'd made things transform into something else, only to have them dissolve into dust moments later. We'd made inanimate objects scream like they'd been speared through with a knife.

But we learned how to glamour. We could start a fire in the fireplace in two seconds flat. We were near masters of telekinesis.

And I started learning alchemy.

It was complicated. Exceptionally complicated. It required rocks and a commitment of the spirit and time. I wasn't sure I fully understood it. Our instructions weren't great.

Nathaniel couldn't get it to work at all. And maybe I could because I had some kind of affinity for earth. But even still, I couldn't get my rocks to stay gold for longer than twenty minutes.

But I was determined. I would do this. I would make this work.

Because I knew my future was shifting. What I thought was my goal no longer was. And I needed to find some way to support us so we could continue our study.

Somehow, I would master alchemy.

When the sun started to drop behind the horizon, Nathaniel and I would leave Asteria House, and walk hand in hand back down the beach. The rest of the day was devoted to our schoolwork. Some nights we studied together. Some we went our separate ways.

The third week in December, we prepared for a different kind of night.

Me and Dad had gone up to Boston the weekend before and went shopping. And tonight, my heart ached for my mother.

She hadn't been there for either of the proms I'd attended in high school. I'd had to get ready on my own and with the help of my father.

She still wasn't here when I was University age. And I still hadn't figured out what had happened to her.

In the bathroom, I wound my hair around the curling iron, being careful not to burn my fingers or my scalp.

"The committee did a really fantastic job this year," my dad said. He sat on the floor in the hallway, his back propped up against the wall. He was barefoot, even though it was freezing in the house. His ankles were crossed, one on top of the other. He watched me as I got ready. "Your mother would have loved it."

I looked over at him, hating that we had to miss her like this. I hated that she was gone. And I hated that we still didn't know why.

"You know it's not nice to tease," I said, looking back in the mirror. "Or to spoil surprises."

"Aren't both of those things part of my job description as a father?" he asked with a laugh.

"Endless support and undying devotion," I corrected him.

"Oh, I think I nailed that part when I paid for that dress, Margot," he said, raising his eyebrows.

I blushed at myself in the mirror. I knew I had things easy. I didn't have to go get a job. My father reiterated all the time that he was happy to have me live at home, and so long as I helped with the grocery shopping and cooking, he'd front the costs. I had it good and easy. So long as I didn't mind living with him.

Which I didn't.

I wasn't sure when I would ever feel good about moving out and leaving him entirely alone.

"Alright," I said as I unplugged the iron. I looked myself over one last time. My hair was pretty fantastic if I did say so myself. My makeup was done to the very best of my ability. "I'm going to put my dress on now. Zip me up in a minute?"

My father gave a little smile and nodded.

I stepped out of the bathroom, and carefully stepped over him and closed myself in my bedroom.

My dress was red satin with a V cross neck across my bust. The sleeves slipped off my shoulders. The waist was narrow before billowing out into a full skirt.

I slipped into it, zipping it up as far as I could

manage. I turned to the full-length mirror that hung on the back of my door and admired myself.

It made my waist look narrow and my hips full. It accentuated my bust in all the right ways and highlighted my collar bones. I'd curled my hair back and then taken two strips into a twist at the back of my head.

I smiled, just thinking of Nathaniel's reaction at seeing me.

I opened the door and found Dad waiting.

His eyes got red the second he saw me. He covered his mouth with a hand and just stood back for a second.

"If you can't handle seeing me in this dress, how are you ever going to handle a white one?" I teased him.

"You trying to tell me something?" he asked. His voice was rough but playful.

I shook my head, but the thought made my heart flutter.

I was only nineteen. I couldn't think about getting married.

Even though I had. On more than a few occasions since I'd met Nathaniel Nightingale.

I turned on the spot and my father zipped me up the rest of the way.

"I will admit," he said as I turned to face him again. "It was well worth the money."

I smiled and wrapped my arms around him. "Thank you, again. It's all that I could have imagined."

He pressed a kiss to my forehead and just then there was a knock at the door.

"Wait here," Dad said with a wink. "You never did the grand staircase reveal for any of the other events."

I just laughed and shook my head at him, but I waited at the top of the stairs while he ran down the stairs to open the door.

I placed my hands over my stomach at the sound of Nathaniel's voice. It was suddenly full of butterflies. And I couldn't stop smiling as I imagined him in a tuxedo. Softly, he and my father talked for a minute.

Maybe there was some cue I was supposed to wait for. But we hadn't discussed it.

So finally, I couldn't wait anymore. I stepped down the first stair and then the next.

Slowly, one step at a time, my view of Nathaniel grew. First, shiny shoes. Then, well fit trousers. A clean and pressed jacket. A black bowtie.

And then him. His tamed hair, which he'd left long for my benefit. His eyes were wide and sparkled. His mouth was slightly slack.

He looked awe struck.

And I felt the same.

He looked like a ruler. He looked powerful. He looked capable of anything in that tux.

I found myself grinning like a fool, and I didn't care one bit.

"You okay, Nathaniel?" my dad asked, staring at my boyfriend with real concern.

Nathaniel's mouth closed, but he only nodded. He stepped forward, meeting me at the bottom of the stairs.

He reached out a hand, wrapping it around my waist and pulling me to meet his lips.

The kiss may have appeared chaste, for my father's sake. But it reached down into my stomach, all the way to my toes. It ignited every spark of desire in me.

"You look incredible, Margot," Nathaniel said as he pulled away and rested his forehead to mine.

"I'm not sure how I'm going to make it through the night with you looking like that," I whispered to him, knowing he could read the hunger in my eyes.

"I'm going to be a grandpa by next Halloween," I heard my dad mutter from behind us.

Nathaniel stepped away from me and I just fixed Dad with a look and shook my head. I really debated telling him right then and there that we still hadn't even had sex yet. But I didn't want either of us blushing that hard.

"How about you just take the picture so we can be on our way?" I asked.

He nodded and grabbed the camera from the kitchen counter.

It really was like high school again. Nathaniel and I posed in front of the bay window, his arm around my waist, my hand on his chest. Dad snapped half a dozen pictures and finally we stepped outside on our own.

I was really thankful the snow had stopped falling. I didn't need it ruining my hair.

"That dress is going to be a problem tonight," Nathaniel said once we were out of earshot of the house.

"What?" I asked in offense. "This dress is amazing."

Nathaniel looked down at me and there was a playful smirk on his face. "I know. And I can't decide if it's better on or if I'm going to be able to keep myself from ripping it off of you."

"Nathaniel Nightingale," I said in a chiding tone. "I had pegged you for a gentleman. And here you are, talking about ripping my clothes off."

He pulled me to a stop and wrapped me into a kiss right there. His hand came to the back of my head, his fingers lacing into my hair. His other hand came low on my hip, pulling our bodies together. His kiss was soul entangling. I breathed him in, and he sucked my soul in and out of me. I felt us converging into one.

"Stars, I never knew I could be this happy," Nathaniel breathed into my mouth. He looked into my eyes between desperate gasps for air. And I felt every word he said.

I didn't want to ever untangle from him.

I was ready to start the rest of our lives, right here. Today.

I wanted our forever. Our story.

I looked up at Nathaniel as he pulled away slightly. I felt full. I felt complex and exceptionally simple all at the same time.

"I love you," I confessed right there.

My chest felt ready to explode from how big and true the words were. I felt like I could destroy the whole world with the entirety of the words.

The look in Nathaniel's eyes softened as he looked down at me. He pulled me closer, if that was even possible. Once more, he lowered his lips to mine, but he didn't quite kiss me. They lingered there, so that I could only feel their warmth, not their touch.

"I love you with everything in me, Margot," he said, filling me so full, I could die at any second. "It's kind of painful sometimes how much I love you."

I smiled, because I knew exactly how he felt. But I just wrapped my arms behind his neck and pulled his lips to mine so I could kiss the man I loved.

We were drawing looks, because there were half a dozen other couples headed to the school for the ball. So, with a deliriously happy grin, I grabbed Nathaniel's hand and pulled him toward the doors, taking off at a run.

I was out of breath when we got to the front doors, but I didn't even mind. We stepped through and Nathaniel handed over our tickets. And we followed the crowd of well-dressed students to the common area.

Dad was right. Mom would have loved this. I couldn't stop looking around in wonder.

Somehow the council had transformed the common room into a golden castle of twinkling wonder. There were plants everywhere, and lights were strung back and forth across the ceiling. Golden decorations were set up throughout the space. There were tables set up all around the perimeter of the room, and there were white and gold tablecloths on them with matching candlesticks and candles set up on them.

It was elegant and beautiful and classy.

I took a moment to look at all the other couples around us. It was a fashion show of expensive dresses and elegant hair. Pinks and whites and blue. Twists and curls and pearls. Each dress was unique and elegant.

And I realized that most of the guys cleaned up nicer than expected. I'd never seen them look so dapper and sophisticated. Tuxedos went a long way.

None of them could live up to Nathaniel, though.

He was getting looks. A lot of them. Other women

were looking him up and down, lust and desire in their eyes, regardless if they had another man on their arm.

And I didn't miss the lingering stares in my direction. I was aware how much of my cleavage showed, how touchable my waist looked.

And I loved how Nathaniel's hands hadn't left it since we left the house.

"This way," Nathaniel said as he led us toward the back of the space. He aimed us toward another woman I recognized from the library, Amy. She was nice, if not a little timid. But I smiled as I sat beside her and her date, a man I didn't recognize.

Nathaniel sat beside me and automatically, I found his hand. He leaned in close to me, our bodies angled together, and he tucked a lock of hair behind my ear, his eyes lingering…everywhere.

I felt on fire with love. Nathaniel had been a song I couldn't get out of my head for months, and now he was mine and I was his. The way he looked into my eyes, I just felt it.

Me and him, we were the forever kind of love. The kind of love people wrote stories about, the kind of love others envied and longed for.

And we were here, together.

This was real.

I stood and moved into his lap. I cupped my hands behind his head. There was a peaceful happiness in his eyes as he looked up into my face. I could feel his heart beating without even touching him, because it was the same beat that was in my own chest.

I tipped forward, and I kissed him.

I could spend the rest of my life doing this. I planned to do exactly that.

But the room got nosier and then quieter. I looked up to see everyone had taken their seats.

There, standing at the head table, was David Sinclair.

I'd forgotten where this event originated from. It had been hosted and put on by the Society Boys for over a century.

And as the head of the Society Boys, David Sinclair was in charge.

He wore a tuxedo that was black, but the lapels were trimmed with a gold, shimmery material. I could see it was lined with the same. His bowtie was also ostentatious. And of course, he wore a masquerade mask.

Each of the Society Boys was dressed over the top, showing everyone else up, though not quite to the extent of David. They each looked powerful and supernatural in their masks. They looked like they could conquer the world.

Each of them was accompanied by a beautiful woman. From their dresses to their hair and their makeup, they were perfect. I didn't want to judge a fellow woman, but I wondered if they really thought about the kind of men they were going out with.

I felt a little bit sorry for the woman sitting beside David in her golden dress like a prize won, because even from across the room, David's eyes were fixed on me.

I gave him a little smile and a wink as I slid off of Nathaniel's lap and back into my own seat.

He stood and actually clanged his knife into the side of his glass. The crowd grew quiet, and all eyes turned to him.

"What an evening," he said, plastering on his power sleek smile as he looked around the room filled with over one hundred of our classmates. "I think our decorating committee deserves a round of applause."

He didn't give the specific individuals credit, so as we clapped, we had no idea who we were clapping for, but I appreciated their efforts, regardless.

"Your dinner was prepared by the finest chefs in the state of Massachusetts," David continued. "I hope you'll enjoy it. And when we're done, I hope you'll welcome the Dark Side of Boston."

I had no idea what the Dark Side of Boston was, my only guess was a band. But David took a seat, and instantly, an army of servers appeared out of nowhere, carrying trays with covered plates.

A delighted smile crossed my face as my plate was set in front of me and uncovered.

There was oven roasted chicken and braised carrots, garlic and rosemary potatoes, and heavenly smelling rolls.

Only, when I went to take my first bite, the food was cold.

I looked over at Nathaniel, and as he slowed in chewing his food, I knew that his was the same.

I looked up and around to be sure that no one was looking. When I confirmed that they weren't, I reached up and rubbed my hands together. I snapped my fingers, and touched the tip of my plate.

There was a quick, small flash.

And when I took another bite, my food was piping hot.

Nathaniel smiled knowingly as he did the exact same.

It was a lovely meal, but the real excitement came when the band came in. As couples finished, they made their way into the middle of the room and things got a little crazy as the dancing started.

I swallowed my last bite just as Nathaniel stood and extended a hand out for mine. With a smile, I took it, and followed him out into the middle of the room.

The music was…exciting. Music wasn't a big part of our house at home, and I only occasionally listened to the radio. But the lead singer's voice was epic. His pitch was phenomenal. The guitars, the drums. It was all spectacular.

As a slower song came on, I looped one hand behind Nathaniel's neck, and he tilted his forehead down to touch mine. He put his hands on either side of my waist, and I swear with this dress, his fingertips nearly touched together. I let my other hand rest against his chest.

We swayed back and forth together, and I relished in the moment. This was the happiest day of my life.

I'd told Nathaniel that I loved him, and he'd returned those words. We were infinite in this moment and it felt like the future would be absolutely perfect.

"Did I tell you, you look incredible?" Nathaniel whispered against my cheek. Softly, his hands trailed up the backs of my arms, sending a wave of goosebumps flashing over my skin.

"You might have mentioned it," I said softly.

He gently kissed my jaw, trailing his lips along my skin. "I think I want to spend the rest of my life with you, Margot Bell. You and those five to twelve children. Together, in Asteria House."

I looked up into his eyes. I felt his words. I felt them all the way down into my heart.

He meant what he said. It wasn't exactly a proposal. It was too soon, we were too young, and we still had too much to accomplish. But I could tell his statement was real.

"Then stick around, forever," I said.

He leaned down and pressed his lips to mine, and it was sealed with a kiss.

I lay my head on his chest, and slowly, we swayed to the music.

I was entirely happy and content.

Until we turned, and I met eye to eye with David.

He danced with his woman who clung to him like she was a child and he her prize. But he stared at me and glared at Nathaniel with a heat that was almost frightening.

I didn't glare. I didn't make faces. I just held his gaze. I let him look at me. I let him see how happy I was.

I hoped he understood. He was never going to buy my affection or sway me to his side with offers of power.

I turned my head to the other side, and I looked away.

Twenty minutes later, we'd worked our way to one corner of the room. "I'll be right back," Nathaniel said as he handed me a glass of cider. "I'm just going to use the restroom."

I nodded and sat at a table, letting my feet have a

break. I was glad I'd worn flats, but still, they squeezed my feet in an uncomfortable way.

There were a few serious couples at Alderidge. Two of them were even officially engaged, all seniors. But most of these people were just here on singular dates. A few of these people might move into a relationship after this night. But most would go their separate ways after the ball. Nothing would come of this night.

The stories I'd tell about this night someday…

I smiled as I watched one couple dance, doing a dramatic rendition of the Lindy. They looked like they were having fun and didn't care that they were getting strange looks and their dance absolutely didn't fit the music.

"Margot." A voice from the side drew my attention away. It was Nathaniel's friend from the library, Amy. She slipped into the chair beside me and looked around nervously. "Something really bad is about to happen. I just saw Nathaniel walking out of the restroom and…"

She looked around again, nervous as a squirrel in the middle of a dog park.

"Amy," I said, sitting up straight, alarmed at her nervousness. "What happened?"

Once more, she looked around. "He was coming out of the bathroom and then the Society Boys grabbed him."

I shot to my feet. "All of them?" I questioned.

She nodded, her face stark white.

"Did you see where they took him?"

"They were headed down to the trail to the beach," she said.

My heart was in my throat. All of my insides were white hot.

Without another word, I turned, and sprinted out the door, drawing eyes, and not caring.

CHAPTER EIGHTEEN

THE HALLWAY WAS QUIET AND EMPTY. MY FEET slapped against the tile beneath them as I sprinted down the hallway, holding my dress up so I didn't trip on it.

I slammed into the door that led out the back of the school. My hands and hips barked in pain from the impact, but I didn't care. I bolted outside into the freezing cold.

Snow had started falling again. It landed on my bare shoulders and instantly started melting. But I sprinted across the back lawn of the school, down the path to the archway that led down to the beach.

I heard a yell as I got closer. But it was drowned with the sound of crashing waves.

There they were. All six of them, standing out in the surf, soaking their suits.

And there was Nathaniel in the middle of them. He had his hands held up, and I couldn't hear his words, but I could tell he was trying to talk some sense into them.

But Borden grabbed him from one side, James from the other. And then David stepped forward and took a swing.

A demented scream ripped from me the moment David's fist connected with Nathaniel's jaw.

I went sprinting across the beach.

And watched in horror as David jumped on Nathaniel, taking him down into the water. The next second, Donald and Howard were on him, too.

I screamed in panic as I watched them push Nathaniel's face under the waves. As they pinned him down while he struggled to save himself from drowning.

I watched blood seep into the water.

Another fist flew. Someone kicked Nathaniel.

My vision went red.

I felt darkness gather in my chest.

My hands grew ice cold.

As I watched David push Nathaniel beneath the waves again, I reached my hands forward, and let loose a savage scream.

Everything blasted back out into the ocean. Sand. Water. And bodies.

David launched into the ocean, as did Borden and James. Donald, Gerald, and Howard went spiraling back out into the ocean with a force that left their bodies limp like rag dolls.

But I hardly even noticed.

I sprinted out into the water, and barely managed to keep my balance as I grabbed Nathaniel, trying to pull him up before the next wave could fill back in.

He gasped and coughed and looked around with wild, blood-red eyes. Already, his right eye was swelling shut and there was a cut on his left cheek. His lip was split again. And the way he was clutching his left side, I had to wonder if his ribs were broken.

"We need to get you to a hospital," I said, nearly shouting to be heard above the noise of the waves and the storm.

"What…where are they?" Nathaniel breathed out.

But he stumbled. He nearly went down in the water again.

"Nathaniel!" I said, fear spiking in the back of my brain again.

He staggered in the surf.

I looped his arm around my shoulders and dragged him up onto the beach as quick as I could.

And as soon as we were out of harm's way, Nathaniel collapsed.

"No, no, no!" I cried as I tried to position us better. I knelt in the wet sand and pulled Nathaniel's head into my lap. I shook him, I cried his name, but he wouldn't wake up.

The sound of coughing drew my eyes back to the ocean.

Donald walked up the beach, coughing mass amounts of sea water from his lungs.

He was followed by Borden. And then David.

They could hardly walk. They nearly crawled as they trudged out of the sea.

I wasn't even sure if Nathaniel was still alive.

And they'd done this to him.

I felt something dark coiling inside of me. It was hot and cold at the same time. It came from a dark, deep place inside of my body, my soul.

The world shifted. It twitched.

My palms felt icy.

James came sloshing out of the ocean, and then was followed by Howard.

They tried to kill Nathaniel, who wouldn't fight back, because he knew what he was capable of.

David met my eyes. And I'd never hated anyone in my life. Not truly. But I hated David then.

I wanted him to suffer. I wanted him to pay.

They were halfway up the beach. They looked exhausted. They looked half drowned.

But I didn't care.

David took one more step toward me.

I raised a hand.

And something that looked like embers from a fire shot out from it. Like a ripple across the water, it fanned out.

And the second it hit them, they each collapsed to the ground.

For just a moment, I sat there stunned and frozen. Until I watched David's chest, and it rose and fell. Each of them were still breathing.

And it was then that I realized that Gerald had yet to come out from the ocean.

My eyes scanned the horizon, but there were no signs of him.

"Margot?" a scared voice called.

My head whipped back, and I watched as Amy came running out to the arch, her date in tow.

"Call 911!" I screamed to her, praying she could hear me across the beach.

Her eyes found Nathaniel lying in my lap, and the five other boys laying sprawled on the sand. She turned and ran back to the school.

Turning my attention back to Nathaniel, my heart broke out into a sprint again. I tried to remember the babysitting training I'd done years and years ago, on how to check for a pulse and how to do CPR.

I pressed my fingers into the side of his neck and waited.

His pulse was there, but it didn't feel strong to me.

I tore his suit jacket open and yanked his shirt up.

A massive bruise was already spreading on his left side. What did that mean? Internal bleeding?

This was bad. I didn't know anything about medical care, but I knew Nathaniel wasn't good.

Tears sprang into my eyes and my heart plummeted into the souls of my feet.

I couldn't let him die. We had our entire lives to live. We'd just promised it. We were finally at our beginning.

I couldn't let him die.

We'd read nothing about healing magic. I didn't even know if it was possible.

But I placed my hand on Nathaniel's chest, and I willed him to live. I imagined all the injuries inside of him and I pictured them healing. I begged his body to tap into his magical blood and heal itself. I pleaded for his lifeforce to stay inside of him.

The waves continued to crash. It started snowing harder. The wind was picking up.

I was ice cold. But I felt nothing.

I willed Nathaniel to live, because I loved him, and he deserved to live.

As I heard the sound of sirens approaching, I looked down at Nathaniel's ribcage. The bruising wasn't gone, but it was less. And I could actually see his chest rising and falling.

He wasn't waking up, but I thought it was better.

It was chaos. Paramedics and police swarmed the beach, and with the noise and commotion, dozens of students flooded to the shoreline, watching.

They all peppered me with questions. Who was injured the worst? Nathaniel. What happened?

I had to think quick, because I couldn't logically explain it all.

They were drunk. Out of their minds. They'd been beating Nathaniel up. Most of them were already passed out when I got down here. I pulled Nathaniel away from them. Maybe they were on drugs, because they all went down like flies.

The paramedics whisked them all away in ambulances, two to each.

I tried to go with Nathaniel, but the police stopped me.

"We're going to need you to come down to the station and give an official statement," one of the officers said, holding a hand up in front of me, standing between me and the retreating ambulance.

"Please," I begged. "My boyfriend, he doesn't have any family. I'm all he has. I need to be with him."

"Ma'am," the officer said, losing his patience. "You'll see him soon. But first, you need to tell us what happened after you've calmed down."

As I watched the ambulance with Nathaniel in it disappear, my father appeared on the grass above me.

"Dad, go to the hospital with Nathaniel!" I said, panic and relief flooding into me. "Please! Don't make him be alone!"

"Where are you going?" he asked. I could see the fear in his eyes, the panic. He'd done this dance before, being questioned for something he hadn't done.

Except I did do this.

"We need to take her in for questioning about what happened here," the officer explained.

I saw the fight surge in my father's eyes. I saw him draw in a breath.

"Dad, please," I begged before he could say anything. "Go be with Nathaniel. I'll be fine."

He didn't like it. I knew he'd do anything for me, he'd fight any battle I asked.

But he knew me. He knew what I really needed right then.

So he nodded, and he turned, and ran back for the car.

"Let's go," I said, in a rush to get this over with so that I could go be with Nathaniel.

Almost everyone who was inside at the ball was now out watching the drama. Who could stay away with the flashing lights and the retreating sound of sirens? When there were six unconscious men on the beach, and they didn't even know that Gerald still hadn't emerged from the water.

Was he dead?

Did I drown him?

I didn't know, and my brain couldn't process that right then.

With dozens of eyes watching me—the deranged girl with a sea-soaked ball gown and her hair covered in snow—I walked up the path and climbed into the back of the police car parked right on the grass.

CHAPTER NINETEEN

The officers got in with me, and I didn't look at my peers as we drove off.

I wasn't afraid until we were pulling into the police station. And then I started remembering Mare McGregor. I remembered the way the witch trials started around the globe. With events that couldn't be explained. With women who could do things that didn't make sense.

How many of my kind had died? Because they'd lost their shit and done things that exposed them?

My hands were shaking uncontrollably by the time the officers parked in front of the station, and not just because I was nearly frozen solid. My stomach had disappeared. I could hardly see straight.

So, as they opened the door and let me out, I took a deep breath. I held my head high. And walked inside.

They brought me a blanket and wrapped it around my shoulders, because I couldn't stop shivering. One kind secretary even brought me a cup of hot chocolate to try and thaw me out.

And then I told my story very calmly.

I told them how David had been pursuing me relentlessly for weeks, nearly to the point of stalking. I told them I'd explained that I was very happy with Nathaniel, but David seemed determined to change my mind.

I told them how I'd seen the five of them acting strangely earlier in the night. That at first, I'd thought they were just drunk. But they weren't just acting drunk. They were acting violent, dark.

I was lying. I knew lying was bad.

But these were the most powerful boys in the school.

I knew their rich and powerful parents would get them out of any trouble I could get them in.

I knew these cops would believe me, even if they knew that there was no way they could hold these boys to anything.

So, I lied. I said I thought they were on drugs.

And then I told some truth. How they all

disappeared. How a friend came and told me that she'd seen the Society Boys take Nathaniel out of the school against his will. I told the police how I'd ran down to the beach and seen them beating Nathaniel and trying to drown him.

And I elaborated my story of them passing out.

How some of them were already down when I got to the beach. How they were stumbling all over and blinking a million times a minute. How they could barely talk. I told them I'd dragged Nathaniel away from them. And how they'd collapsed.

And then they arrived.

"So, what are you going to do about them?" I asked, even though I already knew the answer. "They tried to drown Nathaniel."

The police officers looked at each other and I watched a silent conversation pass between their eyes. And I knew. They knew.

There would be no punishment. Not with families like the Sinclairs involved. The Richards. The Stewarts.

"We will be interviewing all the boys when they're treated and stable," the first one said. "We'll follow standard procedure."

But we all knew that would lead to nothing.

I just nodded. I knew, I'd still be on my own. That I'd have to handle the Society Boys myself.

"Am I free to go now?" I asked. My voice was

hoarse by this point. I didn't know if they believed me and my lies. I thought they did. But I was tired. All the adrenaline had drained out of my body. And I just wanted to see Nathaniel.

Once more, they looked at each other, and in that wordless conversation between them, I found my exoneration. They nodded.

"We'll give you a ride to the hospital," one said. "We'll need to talk to those boys as soon as possible."

"Thank you," I said numbly.

I didn't even remember walking back out into the snow or getting into their car. I didn't remember the drive to the hospital.

Just that suddenly I was walking into the doors of the emergency room. I was asking for Nathaniel's room number. There were white halls. And then a door with a number.

I stepped in, and tears immediately welled in my eyes as I took in Nathaniel, lying in that hospital bed.

He was awake. He looked over at me immediately. His eye was completely swollen shut now. There were stitches in his cheek. I think they'd glued his lip closed.

He wore no shirt, and his ribs were all taped up.

Tears instantly started streaming down my face. I stepped across the room and wrapped my arms around him. Silently, I sobbed into his chest.

His hand came to the back of my head. He kissed

the top of my head. But he didn't say anything. And for that I was grateful. He knew that I just needed to hold him and feel that he was real.

"What happened at the station?" my dad asked from his chair in the corner of the room.

"I told them what I could," I said as I turned my head and rested my cheek against Nathaniel's bare chest. "I lied about the rest."

"Did they believe you?" he asked. His words were quiet and shook just slightly. He was remembering what he'd gone through with my mother's investigation.

Finally, I stood, but I took one of Nathaniel's hands in mine. "I think so. But they know they won't be able to punish the Society Boys. Their families are too powerful."

My father just shook his head, his expression filled with disgusted anger.

Nathaniel opened his mouth to say something, but just then a doctor walked in. He smiled in my direction but looked down at Nathaniel's chart.

"Your x-ray results are back," he said. "You do have one broken rib. And it looks like you've broken another recently that's just barely healed?"

Nathaniel's brows furrowed in confusion.

But I squeezed his hand.

"Yes," I answered for him.

The doctor nodded. "The internal damage should have been much worse, considering the break. You're lucky. Sometimes the internal bleeding can get into your lungs. You can actually drown on your own blood."

I swallowed once as Nathaniel squeezed my hand. He finally understood.

The Society Boys had broken two of Nathaniel's ribs. They'd caused massive internal bleeding. No wonder he could hardly breathe.

But I'd put my hands on Nathaniel.

I didn't know how to heal. So I hadn't been able to completely heal him.

But I'd stopped him from dying and healed one rib.

"You'll need to restrict activity for the next six weeks," the doctor continued, looking up at Nathaniel. "Little bending and twisting. Your rib will heal up, but you need to be cautious since there isn't any kind of casting we can do for it. Icing it helps. Your lip should close up within a week. Those stitches will need to be taken out in six days. And the swelling in your eye will go down within a few days."

The doctor stepped toward the door. "We'll keep an eye on you for another hour to be sure there's not a concussion. But you'll be home tonight."

"That's it?" I questioned. Nathaniel would have died! And they were sending him home in the same night?

"That's it," the doctor said with a nod. And then he was gone.

I shook my head. I was angry and scared and unsure about what was going to happen.

"You saved him, Margot," my father said softly, pulling me out of my spiral.

I looked at him. He looked proud. And worried, because he was a historian and he was just as aware of what had happened to the past mages as Nathaniel and I were. But he looked proud.

I looked back at Nathaniel.

He squeezed my hand again. "My shield maiden in a bloody gown."

Looking down at myself, I really was a mess. Nathaniel's blood was all over the front of the dress. And the bottom half of it was stained with saltwater, white ring lines all over it.

I laughed, more tears falling down my face, and shook my head.

"This has been the craziest night of my life," I said, looking up at the ceiling. "From the best, to one of the absolute worst."

My eyes flicked to the door, where I saw the police

walking down the hall, asking for Borden Stewart's room.

"So, uh, we better get our stories straight," I whispered.

I told Nathaniel and my father everything I'd told the police. We lined up all the details and were just finishing when the same officers who had driven me here stepped into the room.

"Nathaniel Nightingale," one said. "We're sorry to hear you've been injured. If you're feeling well enough, we'd like to ask you some questions. We're still waiting for all the other boys to wake up."

And something sparked in me. Now that I had magic, I had so many things to think of. I had exposed myself, in so many ways.

I'd blasted them out into the ocean. I'd knocked them out with some dark sparks that came from my hand.

What if they remembered all of that?

I looked down at Nathaniel. I held his eyes, hoping and praying that he understood what I had to do as I bent down to kiss him. I didn't know if he understood, but I saw that he trusted me. He gave just one little nod.

"We'll wait outside," I said, nodding for my dad to get up. And he didn't hesitate as he stood, and walked with me outside of the room, and pulled the door closed behind him.

"What if they remember?" I said in a whispered hiss as we walked down the hall a few paces. "What I did to them? They might say something, and most people wouldn't believe them, but they come from powerful families."

I watched Dad's eyes widen and fear spark in his eyes. He looked up and down the hall. "So, what? We run? Disappear?"

I pulled back, looking into his face with shock. "No," I said. "I make it so they can't remember a damn thing."

I think it really hit Dad then. What I was. What I could do. What his wife could do.

He got really pale.

He looked a little scared.

But in the end, he took my hand, and he nodded.

We walked down the hall, and thankfully, just in the very next room, we found Howard Starrling.

Dad kept watch while I walked up to Howard's bed. He slept peacefully. Maybe not peacefully. I had no idea what I'd done to him.

I'd only briefly read through the book when we were sorting through them. A book on altering or stealing memories. So, I had no idea how to do this correctly.

But I stepped up beside him. I placed my fingertips to the temples of his head, and I let my eyes slide closed.

I pulled up my recollection of a few hours ago. And I listened.

There was an echo in Howard. And suddenly what I was seeing was from his perspective. Everything was funny and he was happy to make Nathaniel pay for being such a weirdo. He'd kicked Nathaniel and pushed his face under the water.

Hot rage flared through me, turning the memory red.

And with it, I saw cracks forming in the memory.

So, I grabbed them, and I twisted them.

I put it in Howard's mind that they'd taken something just before dinner. Something to make the night fun. Things started getting a little hazy and black as the night went on.

I showed him passing out face down into the sand after taking a few swings at Nathaniel, and then black.

My eyes slid open and I looked at Howard as I let go of him.

He slept peacefully.

And now I just had to hope that he remembered things the way I told him to.

One by one, I walked to each room. I visited Donald. I went to James.

And to my exceptional relief, just before I slipped into Borden's room, some doctors went running into a room with a gurney, Gerald Paulson lying on it.

He was alive.

I didn't kill him.

I visited Borden. I told him to believe what I put in his mind.

And then I moved on to David.

I closed the door behind me as I stepped inside. Which maybe was a bad idea. I had some very dark and violent feelings toward him. But I had to do this.

He lay there still and quiet. No leering stares, no smirks, no look of violence in his eyes as he swung a fist at Nathaniel.

He was just a boy.

But that wasn't really the case.

I touched my fingertips to his temples. I closed my eyes. And I aligned my memories with his to find them.

I planted the drugs in his mind. I made the night get blurry and dark. I made sure he blacked out just after I started running down the beach, his last memory of me screaming for him to stop.

And I planted seeds. Seeds of letting me go. Seeds of understanding that he and I would never happen. Seeds of Nathaniel being invisible to him.

That's all I needed. For Nathaniel to be invisible to David. I just wanted David to leave him alone.

And then it was done.

I was proud of myself as I let him go and took a step away. I hadn't killed him. I hadn't planted thoughts of torture and massive guilt in his mind. I didn't think I could. While I didn't know the extent of my own abilities yet, I really didn't think I could entirely alter a person's being. I couldn't make David into a nice or generous person. I couldn't turn him around and make him friends with Nathaniel.

But I hoped the seeds would grow into something that made our lives easier.

Because even though he should go to jail for attempted murder and aggravated assault at the least, I knew he wouldn't. He'd show back up at Alderidge on Monday for finals. He'd be back to finish his final semester after Christmas break.

I once told David that if he ever touched Nathaniel again, that I'd get him kicked out of school. But I realized now that I'd been wrong. I'd been naive. Even though Dean Lowell was a friend, he could still be bought.

David wasn't going to disappear from our lives for at least another four months.

So all I could do was make our lives easier.

I just had to hope it worked.

I turned, and I walked out of the room.

"You okay?" Dad asked. "You're white as a sheet."

And as he asked, I realized how tired I was. I staggered forward to a chair in the hallway and sat on it. "Yeah," I said, feeling a little out of breath. "Just tired. I guess this stuff takes a lot out of me."

My father sat next to me, taking my hand in his. He rubbed soothing circles into it, while I rested my head on one hand, and looked down the hall to the room where they worked on Gerald.

I wasn't done. As soon as they were done stabilizing him, I had to get in there and adjust his memories, too.

So, for another twenty minutes, we watched. The police came out of Nathaniel's room and looked into Howard's. And he must have been awake, because they slipped inside and closed the door halfway.

Immediately, I sprang from my seat and walked quietly to the door.

I listened.

And my heart raced as Howard gave a shameful, half lie account about what happened earlier in the night. He said that maybe they'd had too much to drink. That David had gotten sick of Nathaniel gloating "some girl" in his face and decided to teach him a lesson. And maybe they'd had more than just a drink, because he blacked out on the beach and didn't remember anything else beyond throwing one punch.

Nothing about me blasting them out into the ocean. Nothing about me blacking them out.

I put my hand over my heart, and a small smile pulled on my lips.

It worked.

I'd done it. Even without knowing the right method, I'd reached inside myself and found a way.

My eyes lifted to my father, and I wasn't quite sure how to read the expression in his eyes. He was relieved. But I thought I might have also seen a little bit of disappointment there. And fear.

I understood why.

I hated it.

But I couldn't regret it.

I watched as the doctors slipped out of Gerald's room and after waiting thirty seconds, I slipped inside his room, and I altered his memory as well.

By the time I was done, I was so tired my father had to help me back into Nathaniel's room.

"What's wrong?" Nathaniel asked, sitting up straight, only to lay back down with a pained wince and a hand held over his ribs.

"I'm fine," I said, shaking my head as I dropped down into one of the chairs. "It…it worked. They don't remember what really happened."

Nathaniel looked at me for a moment, and slowly, I saw pride dawning in his eyes.

Nathaniel would fight his battles in his own way. But I would tear down the world to protect him.

A nurse walked in then. "We're ready to discharge you," she said.

There were five minutes of fuss and half a dozen pages signed, then Nathaniel was pulling his blood-stained shirt back on, and he was wheeled back to the front doors. I stood by his side while Dad pulled the car around to the doors. Carefully, the two of us helped Nathaniel into the front passenger seat.

"You're staying with us for a while," Dad said as soon as his door was closed, and the car was in gear. "I can't let you go back to that solarium only to pass out and die. Someone needs to keep an eye on you."

"Arthur, I appreciate it, but—"

"This isn't up for debate, Nathaniel," Dad cut him off. "You're family now. And family takes care of each other."

Nathaniel didn't say anything else. He stared forward, and I watched in the rear-view mirror as a smile pulled in the corners of his mouth, and his eyes got red and welled. "Thank you."

None of us said anything else in the five minutes it took to drive back to the house. Dad parked in the driveway, and again, we helped Nathaniel into the house. And then it was up the stairs.

"I must be the worst father in the world for letting

you do this," my dad said as we made our way into my bedroom. "But I don't think he should be left alone. So you watch him, Margot. I'm not as worried about you making my grandbabies tonight."

I blushed, and laughed, and shook my head. But I was thankful he was such a levelheaded and understanding man. He ducked out of the room and returned a moment later with a set of sleeping clothes for Nathaniel to borrow.

"Thank you, Arthur," Nathaniel said from where he sat on the bed with a nod. "For everything. I really appreciate you. And your acceptance."

I didn't expect it when my father stepped forward and hugged Nathaniel. He held on to him for a good thirty seconds, saying nothing. Just showing Nathaniel that he loved him. That he was sorry Nathaniel had to go through what he did. But that he was home now. He was with family.

And Nathaniel clung to my father with his one good arm. He held him tight. And I could feel it. Nathaniel meant every word he'd said to my father, down to his soul.

"Get some rest," Dad finally said as he stepped back. "Come get me if you need anything."

"Thanks, Dad," I said quietly as I watched him walk out the door.

Nathaniel and I stared at each other without saying

anything for several long moments. Tonight had been terrifying. So many things went wrong and could have gone worse.

Yet here we were, together. Alive. Safe.

I *was* going to get in the shower. I was going to wash the blood off of me and go warm up.

But I just didn't have the energy.

So, I turned my back to Nathaniel, and like he could read my mind, he unzipped my ruined dress. With my back still turned to him, I zipped it down the rest of the way, and stepped out of it. I knew he could see everything in my black underwear and strapless bra. But I didn't glance back as I looked around for a sleeping shirt. I found one in a drawer and pulled it over my head.

I turned to find Nathaniel trying to unbutton his shirt. I crossed to help him, and I felt him studying my face as I undid them one by one. But neither of us said anything. I peeled off his shirt, and when I went to pull on my father's sleeping shirt, he shook his head.

"Anything touching it hurts," he admitted.

And so I left it off.

I helped him pull his shoes off and I helped him peel his ruined slacks off, until he was just in his underwear.

And then I helped him lay in my bed, which

looked so painful. And then I turned out the light and crawled under the covers beside him.

I reached a hand up, laying it on his bare chest. He covered my hand with his, pressing my still-freezing palm into his warm skin.

"Thank you for saving me, Margot," he whispered in the dark.

I leaned forward and gently pressed my lips to his split one. "Always," I promised.

CHAPTER TWENTY

As I'd predicted, every single one of the Society Boys were back at school on Monday. They took their finals, along with everyone else. There were no police. There was no further investigation.

Students whispered about it at school. No one really knew what happened, because it had only been the eight of us on the beach. There were plenty of theories. None of them were quite right.

But maybe my seeds worked.

David simply looked at the two of us from across the halls or the common area. He looked confused. He looked dark.

But he stayed away.

As did all the other Society Boys.

I had two finals that day. I didn't expect to do well,

considering everything that had happened over the weekend, distracting from studying. But when my final grade came back, I got an A in Latin and an A- in Writing.

Nathaniel aced both of his finals that day.

And the ones over the next three days.

I got a B in physical education, but it was really difficult to care about that. I got an A in World Geography.

When the last final was taken and the final grades posted, I walked back to the solarium, hand in hand with Nathaniel with a lot on my mind.

"Something wrong?" Nathaniel asked.

My gaze shifted up, tracing the roofline of all the houses, even though I wasn't really seeing them. "Learning what we have, having gone through all of… this… I didn't think my priorities were ever a question, but things are just different."

Nathaniel looked down at me with confusion. His poor eye was still mostly swollen shut. The stitches stood out in stark contrast against his skin. But with that one good eye, I could see worry.

"I've always had my future planned out, ever since I was a little girl," I said. "I was going to go to Alderidge and then become a professor here."

"But now the plan is changing?" Nathaniel asked for clarification.

I stopped on the sidewalk, looking up at Nathaniel. "I guess it just feels like I might be needed more elsewhere," I said. "What we've discovered, it's big. I feel like this could be my study, my life's work. Learning magic and bringing it back from extinction. What good is getting a typical university degree, when I know my path no longer lies in being a professor?"

Nathaniel brushed his thumb over the back of my hand. "I understand what you're saying. It makes perfect sense to me. And I think you're right about our paths being different from what we thought they would be just six months ago. You're not one to do what's expected of you, Margot. If you're done with Alderidge, go with your gut."

I actually huffed a laugh and shook my head. "I didn't really expect you to just make this so easy," I said with a sigh as we continued back down the path to the solarium. "You're one of the hardest working students I know. You worked your butt off just to get in on that scholarship. You're really okay with it if I just drop out?"

"I would never get it in my head to tell you what to do, Margot," he said as we turned the corner around the fence and started down the overgrown path. "I saw what you did to the Society Boys on the beach."

I laughed and shook my head. But immediately I sighed. "I'm going to stick it out for one more semester," I said. "I think in the end Dad would understand, but I think he'd be disappointed that I couldn't finish one whole year. And I think I need to prove it to myself."

We stepped inside the solarium and we both hung our jackets on the coat hook.

And still being gentle to not overdo it, Nathaniel wrapped his hands around my waist and pulled me to him. I placed my hands on his chest, being delicate and cautious.

"Whatever you choose, Margot, I know you're going to amaze me every day," he said, locking with my eyes. "I'm just honored you're letting me come along for the ride."

A smile crossed my lips. I brought my hands to the back of his head, and I guided his lips down to mine.

CHAPTER TWENTY-ONE

The day after Christmas, Nathaniel and I spent a lazy day in the solarium. He was dressed in the sweater I'd bought him. I wore the necklace he'd gotten me. We were lying on the couch and the fire was roaring. We were both enjoying the lazy days between semesters. They wouldn't last long.

"I think we should go back to your mother's office and find that book," Nathaniel said as I turned the pages of a different book. "The memory altering could probably have saved a lot of other mage's lives. Seems like an important skill to have."

I rolled onto my back, looking up at Nathaniel's face. "Once the break is done," I said. "I'm not setting foot back inside that school sooner than I have to."

Nathaniel chuckled and leaned down and

kissed me.

And then he sat bolt upright when there was a knocking sound against glass.

I stood up, Nathaniel right after me.

Through the organized, beautiful chaos of the solarium, we saw Borden Stewart at the door. He stared at us through the glass, snow falling onto his head and shoulders.

Instantly, I felt my palms grow hot.

Cautiously, Nathaniel went to the door and opened it.

"What do you want, Borden?" I asked in a growl as I stepped beside Nathaniel.

There was something I'd never seen in the Society Boy's eyes before. He looked uncertain, maybe even nervous.

"I need to talk to you, Margot," he said. He looked nervous. Worried about Nathaniel, but even more nervous about me.

"You can go tell David that nothing has changed," I said, crossing my arms over my chest. "He needs to go find a new pretty toy."

"It's not about David," Borden said in a quick tone. "It's about what happened on the beach."

My eyes widened just a bit and I looked at Nathaniel.

"The Boys keep trying to figure out who brought

the drugs, who got us into this mess," Borden said. He looked from me, to Nathaniel, and back to me again. "And I can't figure out what the hell they're talking about. We didn't take any drugs that night. None of us were even drinking."

My heart started racing faster.

"But I remember you," he said, fixing me with his eyes. "I remember you screaming like a banshee. I remember flying through the air and into the ocean."

My heart was drumming in my ears now.

"I remember walking out of the water, and something coming out of your hands, and then black." Borden's words grew darker by the moment.

Something like fear and dread and excitement grew in my veins.

"I don't know what you did to the Boys to make them forget, to make them think something totally different happened," Borden said. "They all think they did drugs and passed out on the beach right when you ran out." He shook his head. "But I know what really happened."

"You were high," Nathaniel said, shaking his head. The evidence of their beating was still all over his face. "Go home to your castle, Borden."

Borden shot a hand out to stop Nathaniel from closing the door.

And suddenly something blue crackled over his

hand.

Like lightning.

My eyes snapped up to Borden's.

He gazed back at me with a dead serious expression.

I looked back at his hand. The electrical lightning continued to crackle over his hand.

A curse slipped over Nathaniel's lips.

"My entire life, I thought I was alone," Borden said as he removed his hand from the door. There was a black scorch mark, in the exact shape of his land, left on the door. He brought both of his hands up together, and I watched as lightning sparked between them, crackling back and forth. "I thought I was the only freak in the world. Until that day on the beach, when I watched you do two impossible things."

Dread dropped heavy in my stomach.

"Teach me," Borden asked, and there was something in his voice that wasn't just asking. He was begging. "Please," his words came out as a whisper.

But I shook my head. "After what you've done to Nathaniel, you'd dare come and ask us to help you?"

And with my words, I realized I'd just ratted Nathaniel out. Borden's eyes flicked up to meet Nathaniel's. There was understanding that dawned in his eyes.

"You and your boys nearly killed him that day," I

said, disgust dripping from my words. "And you want me to help you?"

"I can only access it when I'm angry," Borden suddenly said, his words coming out in a combined jumbled rush. "Calm and happy, I can't make the lightning happen. But when I'm angry... It's the only reason I stay with the Society Boys, because they piss me off more than any other people on this planet."

His words stunned me silent. I had to blink five, six, seven times as I processed what he'd just said.

"David's an entitled asshole, and I know you think I am, too," Borden said as he tucked his hands back into his pockets to protect them from the cold. "I might be rich, and I'll never escape the royalty reputation around here. But I swear, the only reason I'm with the Boys is so I can have control over this. If you teach me, if you can help me, I swear, I'll never even talk to David again."

His eyes burned with sincerity. They burned so bright I almost forgot that he'd been with the Boys the night they'd tried to kill Nathaniel.

I saw it in his eyes. In his lips. In the arch of his eyebrows.

"The name Stewart is from Scotland," Nathaniel said. "A long line of kings and violence and war. And… more than one accused mages in the area were Stewarts."

I let my eyes slide closed as Nathaniel's words sank down into me.

Borden was one of us. A Society Boy. But also, a mage.

"I swear, Margot," he said, and I hated that I believed him. "If you will help me, I will be loyal to you. And Nathaniel. You will have my resources. And I will make sure David and the rest of the Boys never, ever bother the two of you again."

I opened my eyes, and for the first time, I saw an innocent, scared and confused boy.

I saw a cousin. A brother. An equal.

"Please, Margot," Borden breathed, looking absolutely open and desperate. "Teach me what I am."

Everything in my heart wanted to say no. I didn't want to forgive. I didn't want to trust that he could change like he was promising.

But as I looked up at Nathaniel, I saw in his eyes that he'd already forgiven Borden Stewart. He had hope in his eyes. There was excitement in him.

In that look between us, I saw Nathaniel's answer.

So, with a tight breath in my chest, I looked back at Borden. I met the eyes of a different man. Someone I didn't know. Someone I would have to forgive.

"Alright," I said. "Come inside."

THE END OF BOOK ONE

ABOUT THE AUTHOR

Keary Taylor is the USA TODAY bestselling author of over thirty titles, encompassing paranormal, sci-fi, and contemporary romance. She grew up along the foothills of the Rocky Mountains where, from a young age, she started creating imaginary worlds and daring characters who always fell in love. She now splits her time between a tiny island in the Pacific Northwest and a beautiful valley in Utah, with her husband and their two children. She continues to have an overactive imagination that frequently keeps her up at night.

facebook.com/kearytaylor
twitter.com/kearytaylor
instagram.com/authorkearytaylor

Printed in Great Britain
by Amazon

43550860R00169